'Dare I tell yo[...]
were the hare[...]

Hassan was laugh[...] at her. 'Yes, this place is now my father's home, and these are now my quarters.'

'Even if they are your quarters, they could, I expect, be used for their original purpose.'

Her hand went flying to her mouth as if to hold back the words. She had known this tall, self-assured, arrogant and handsome man for only two days, and she had said that to him. What *had* possessed her? It would serve her right...

Dear Reader

The new year is a time for resolutions and here at
Mills & Boon we will continue to give you the best
romances we possibly can. We're sure the year's books
will live up to your expectations! This month we hope to
shake off the winter chills by taking you to some
wonderful exotic locations—Morocco, the Bahamas and
the Caribbean. Closer to home, this is the time of year
when we celebrate love and lovers, with St Valentine's
Day. Which of our heroes would you like to spend the
day with? Until next month,

The Editor

Mons Daveson grew up on a cattle station in far North
Queensland, but now lives in the famous holiday resort
of Noosa. As she walks beside the ocean she plans the
next chapter of her new novel, which she thoroughly
enjoys doing as she sets her books in such romantic
locations. She has three daughters and two sons, all of
whom are thrilled at her success, and read all her books.

DESERT MAGIC

BY
MONS DAVESON

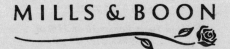

MILLS & BOON LIMITED
ETON HOUSE, 18-24 PARADISE ROAD
RICHMOND, SURREY TW9 1SR

*MILLS & BOON and the Rose Device
are trademarks of the publisher.*

*First published in Great Britain 1994
by Mills & Boon Limited*

© Mons Daveson 1994

*Australian copyright 1994   Philippine copyright 1995
This edition 1995*

ISBN 0 263 78878 4

*Set in Times Roman 10 on 11¼ pt.
01-9502-56137 C*

Made and printed in Great Britain

CHAPTER ONE

THE tall, dark-haired man lounging so indolently against a wall looked up from his copy of the London Times and glanced casually round the terminal, his gaze indifferent as it passed over Alicia. She wasn't even a person as far as he was concerned; more like a piece of furniture blocking what should be an empty space. Oh, well, it was to be expected, she decided. Why should someone like that spare her a second glance?

She knew that she was fairly attractive with that cascade of honey-coloured hair which glinted and rippled to below her shoulders. She knew also that the tanned apricot of her skin made her eyes seem a deeper shade of blue. But a man like that could attract any woman he wanted. Assured, confident, and outstandingly handsome with classically sculptured features, he was the type to turn female heads wherever he went. And he must know it!

Alicia shrugged. Yet she went on studying him, strangely reluctant to turn away. Although this was Athens airport, he didn't look Greek . . .

There was a sudden stir at the entrance. Through the door strode a passenger who showed no passport or papers and who was waved onwards by the security guard with some deference. Behind him there was another man, clad not in a lightweight tropical suit like his companion, but in a white jibbah and a loose enveloping burnous coloured in broad maroon and white stripes. The same colours were in the twisted cord which banded his kaffiyeh.

The tall man straightened and came forward to greet the new arrival.

'Yusef!'

'Hassan!'

There was a burst of animated conversation in a low, soft language which Alicia did not understand, but recognised none the less. So they were Arabs!

A bustle of movement and a burst of noise from a loudspeaker distracted her attention. Were they going to board the plane at last? She turned back to Aunt Em, patiently seated by her side. 'Not long to wait now before we board, I think. I'll take your bag.'

'Good God! Just look at him!'

It was one of the two young girls Alicia had been speaking with earlier. They were archaeology students travelling to Egypt to work on a dig their university was funding.

'Don't, Sally,' begged the quieter one of the two. 'For heaven's sake don't look at them. You know what we were told about Arab customs. It's not polite to ogle men.'

Not polite, but entirely understandable, Alicia thought, as she followed the direction they were looking in. Yusef, the newcomer, was returning their interest with a look of keen appreciation, causing Sally to turn away, blushing furiously.

However, Alicia looked, even if surreptitiously, as she stood by Aunt Em's side. Another apparition had come to join the first one. This man didn't have those classical sculptured features. He *did* have a face that was just as handsome—but on, in so entirely a different way. It was dark, fierce like a hawk.

He also had an attendant who had gone to stand behind him.

'For heaven's sake, Sally,' again came the almost agonised whisper, 'Don't notice them, please!' as her friend looked like doing just that.

'No, don't,' surprised, Alicia heard herself muttering. She had been surrounded by men all her life. They held no terrors for her. However, that young man looked as wild as the bird of prey he resembled. His look, too, was of that same kind, and thankfully she saw the girl beside her turn away as the colour rose to stain her cheeks.

Now if that look had been from the first man, Alicia thought unexpectedly, she might just have returned it. Then she grinned widely at herself. That one wouldn't even see them, never mind acknowledge them. For one long brown finger had been raised, and the Arab-clad man had bent to pick up a briefcase. Why couldn't he have picked it up himself? reflected Alicia contemptuously. For heaven's sake, a flimsy briefcase! Then grinned again at herself. What business was it of hers? she decided, and took Aunt Em's elbow as there came the exodus towards the plane.

The two men were walking towards the first-class steps, aware of no one else, as if they owned the airport and all in it; their attendant also walked—*through* everyone who didn't get out of his way. Oh, well...another country, another behaviour.

On the plane, as she settled Aunt Em into the window seat, Alicia easily dismissed the small encounter from her mind. It had been just like that old cliché of ships passing in the night. She would never see either of them again. Then she decided, sitting down and fastening her own seatbelt, she had more serious things to think about, to worry about. Had she done the right thing? She knew absolutely that she had. Even her grandfather, although not wanting her to go, had made no serious demur—

except for advice. Heavens, the advice... He had been in Egypt once, a long time ago.

'It's not like it was then, Grandfather,' she had interjected. 'That was a million years ago. They will have had to change to live in today's world.'

'Not them, especially the men,' he had exclaimed dogmatically.

'Well, our agent in Cairo is meeting me, and I have to go, you know.' He had nodded then, agreeing. So now she watched the city of Athens and then the port of Piraeus cartwheel beneath them, with a sapphire ocean coming to take their place. She settled down and made herself think of the city they had just left behind them, and then the one she was going to. She intended to see more of both before she went home.

It was still daylight when the announcement came to fasten seatbelts, and Cairo was rushing towards them. Craning across Aunt Em, Alicia even saw the Pyramids— for a brief fleeting second. Oh, well...she intended to see them properly, and also other places in this land she had read so much about...somehow!

The airport when they arrived seemed to close in all about her. It was packed, and, hearing the volume of noise, the incomprehensible speech spoken so loudly everywhere, Alicia acknowledged that she was indeed on alien soil.

She stood with Aunt Em by the luggage carousel, and smiled goodbye to her travelling companions, who told her, 'We're off now, Alicia. Maybe we'll see one another down in Luxor. Bye!'

Watching them depart, young, excited, amid the cheerful group which had met them, Alicia suddenly felt alone, abandoned. They were a part of a culture she knew—while here...

Then passing her she saw the men from the Athens airport, not, like her, waiting mundanely for luggage.

They too were being met. Two Arabs, or Egyptians or whatever, had moved swiftly towards them, clad in now familiar colours. The elder, bearded, greeted first the younger hawk-faced one with the traditional greeting of respect. Then he repeated the gesture towards the man she had first noted in the Athens airport.

Then her attention was abruptly brought back to this alien crowded place, when a voice asked, 'Miss Seacombe?' Alicia swung round to be confronted by a grave, middle-aged Egyptian.

'Yes,' she acknowledged, 'and my aunt, a Miss Seacombe also.'

'I know. I am Mr Hamid, the Egyptian representative of your Australian company. Your luggage?' It was a question.

Alicia gestured to the carousel just as her aunt said, 'There it is.'

A hand was pointed and two porters in their coffee-coloured ankle-length jibbahs bent forward and collected the cases, Alicia bent equally quickly to grab at her overnight case as it went sliding past. It was taken from her. And they went, a small procession through the busy, vociferous crowd, towards a new and so different city. Her attention given entirely to this, and to their agent, Alicia didn't see one pair of eyes look assessingly, not at her, but at her companion.

The cases deposited, she went to tip the men with money obtained in Athens for this very purpose, before hearing Mr Hamid saying in a hard, displeased voice, 'It has already been attended to.'

Alicia turned from smiling at the two porters who were bowing low to her, and encountered a glance being directed for the first time completely upon her; upon her, not as if at some empty space. And she saw eyes suddenly pinpointed with brilliance. Her own gaze held. She could no more look away than move! For the space of a slow heartbeat that glance locked, and sent magnetism like a flowing pulse between them. Then the tableau was shattered. Hooded lids had fallen and the man had turned to enter an opulent black limousine as it moved silently away.

She entered her own vehicle, wondering what, if anything, had happened. She still felt the shock throughout her entire metabolism. But it had been a long day, a long flight. What was it they said about jet lag?

The agent had turned in his seat and was speaking to them about the horses. Alicia nodded and smiled, but she wasn't listening. She also didn't intend to remember a glance from wide-open eyes from which brilliance struck. A glance that had held her spellbound, inescapable, as if joined to it by a twisted invisible cord. So, settling back, she gazed out upon this alien land to see that they were travelling a wide, straight road seemingly going on forever. Egyptians walking along both sides in their ankle-length gowns gave to it also a foreign perception ... an exotic strangeness.

Abruptly, with a surge forward and a slamming on of brakes, they saw they had arrived. Alicia heard her aunt's astringent mutter, and, grinning over at her, said, 'Live dangerously, Aunt Em, in this new land. You're just used to horses.'

The hotel into which their escort ushered them was opulent. Alicia smiled wryly. It would be the Hilton! At the reception desk, on being handed their key, they found they had Mr Hamid even escorting them upstairs. Her eyebrows rose. She would not have thought that they— or their business—was important enough for top management, as he had suggested he was, to be so assiduous.

He stood, hesitating a little outside their open door, as if trying to find words, then said carefully, 'It was very unfortunate about your manager, but as it was a member of the ben Amarna tribe who was responsible...'

'The ben Amarna . . . ?' interrupted Alicia, puzzled.

'Yes. They are one of the great desert tribes, and are very wealthy and powerful. Everybody walks warily around the ben Amarna.'

'But who or what exactly are they?' It was Aunt Em interjecting astringently this time. She had no patience with people one had to walk warily around. 'What do they do? What is their purpose out there at this so-called horse fair. And how did one of them come to injure Johnny?'

'I'm afraid, dear lady, I cannot answer that. No one asks the ben Amarna their business.'

'Then it's about time someone did.' It was Alicia this time. 'And you are in charge of our horses, aren't you, Mr Hamid? They are all insured through your office.'

'Yes, of course . . . but besides that, you need have no worry. No one—native or foreigner—would dare lay even the imprint of a finger upon any of your animals. The ben Amarna has placed them under protection. Now I must go. Miss Seacombe.' He bowed to the older woman, gave just the least inclination to the younger one, and departed.

Alicia hustled Aunt Em inside and slammed shut the door. 'Oh, yes,' she exclaimed, unzipping cases with angry force. 'He's happy about everything. He and his firm are covered. But what about Dark Shadow alone out there in the desert all by himself.'

A low cackle of caustic laughter echoing round the room, swung her round. 'I wouldn't worry about him. No one is going to get on *his* back and ride around the countryside,' came tartly from the old lady. 'And I'm sure Johnny, even if he was in pain, would have seen to that. We'll just go and see what he has to say.'

'No, I'll go, Aunt Em. Because I think a bath and dinner up here would be the best idea for you. OK?'

'Go by yourself? Don't be silly! Why was I brought all this way if you can go traipsing around on your own—and at night-time too?'

'You were brought, my love, because everyone—everyone, mind you—said no one would talk to me, a young, unimportant female. You are here to see that they do! But that is for out in the desert at a horse-fair, not here in civilised Cairo. Look, have first bath, and I'll ring down and order a registered taxi.'

A glance at her wristwatch showed that she had time—it was not quite six. So, switching on the kettle, she made tea. Then, with a cup in her hand, and only silence coming from behind the bathroom door, she slipped out on to the balcony.

There, she reflected, in splendid panorama before her, was the Nile. Merchants had carried their precious cargos on it for over five thousand years; and on its waters armies had sailed to war. But most of all, of course, it could be associated with the golden barges of the Pharaohs! What stories it could tell.

Standing there, finishing such a mundane thing as a cup of tea, she saw as if emerging from another dimension the sails of a felucca. Caught in the passing gleam of a sun setting somewhere behind the dark bulk of the hotel, it could have been a ghost ship in white and silver as it fled past on pewter waters. Suddenly, as if coming events cast their shadow, Alicia felt a shiver pass through her whole body. She turned quickly and went inside, to be enclosed in an ordinary hotel bedroom.

Later, swiftly brushing on eyeshadow, smoothing straight with a little oil the arched, naturally black eyebrows which contrasted so definitely with her fairness, Alicia added a blush-rose lipstick to the sparse make-up she was using. As she was giving a last inspecting glance at the overall result, unexpectedly, out of the blue a dark, handsome, classically sculptured face was superimposed over her shoulder. It was so real as it hovered there that she almost swung round. She shook her head dazedly and the image shattered. She *hadn't* been thinking of him, she told herself wrathfully. She had been thinking of all she had to do.

She heard herself saying, 'I'm just taking a small purse, Aunt Em. I've left passports and cheques in the big bag, OK?' Then, moving towards the door, she grinned over her shoulder, saying, 'Don't dare forget to drink your tea. When I asked if they could manage real tea-leaves in the pot for you, their "Certainly, madam, of course" was so outraged one would have thought that I had been using obscene language on the phone.'

She hurried along the corridor, and down in the lift, and 'Yes,' said the reception clerk, 'Your driver is here, Miss Seacombe.'

A finger pointed, and she went towards the man at the entrance. She smiled hello, and followed the guide to some yards away where his car was parked.

Despite her worry she gazed with enchantment at the scene flashing past. It was not what she had expected, this city of the East she had read so much about. For from where she sat it was the myriad cars which dominated.

She said, at the hospital steps, 'Please call for me at eight o'clock,' and added more sharply when the man only nodded, 'You will be here, won't you? The hotel said...'

'Of course I will be, madam. I am a top guide. I am known!' At least he had returned her tentative smile as he set the car in motion. Oh, well, she thought, how was I to know. All she had wanted was not to be left alone in a teeming city.

At a nurse's desk, she asked for Johnny, but it was only after a murmured conference that she was told, 'He is in the private wing. You go along that corridor, turn right and take the lift to the second floor.'

So she went along, a small frown of worry coming to find its way between her brows. She found she was escorted to a door that was half open. She was smiling over her shoulder to say thank you as she walked inside.

She stopped as if crashing into a brick wall. Or, more likely, somewhere a subconscious thought was telling her, as she had once done, slap-bang into a wide, glass, unyielding door.

CHAPTER TWO

SHE knew him, of course she did. The man from the airport. The man whose gaze she had been unable to break. However, this was a different person altogether. She knew far back in a subconscious dimension that she heard Johnny call her name, but she just stood, rooted to the shining tiled floor.

This man was alien, with not the least indication of anything she could relate to. Alicia turned as Johnny called again. She took the hand he held out to her and clung tightly. She knew she said, 'Even before asking how you are, can I say this was a stupid thing for you to do?'

'Yes indeed, you can say that,' replied the young man she had known for always. Then suddenly, hearing that familiar voice, she was back in the substantial world about her; seeing Johnny's answering grin, the bed upon which he lay, the leg encased in plaster and traction. However, he wasn't answering her about his leg; her hand still clasped tightly within his, he had turned to the other occupant of the room. He said, 'This is the Sheikh Hassan ben Amarna, Alicia. Of the ... people who run the horse-fair, and who have all been so very kind to me.'

Making herself turn, she gazed at the tall man dressed in pristine floating white, with the same pure white kaffiyeh bound in the colours she remembered. How did one greet an Arab prince? She was forestalled.

'Miss Seacombe,' said a voice in English—in public school English.

15

So she only said, 'How do you do?' And wondered if in that almost austere face, so different now with only white muslin holding it close, an eyebrow had risen.

Johnny was speaking, pulling at her hand. 'I told them there was no need for all this,' gesturing around the luxurious private room. 'But——' he looked beseechingly at the two other occupants of it '—there was a man here, when I came out of the anaesthetic, who only gave orders . . . who wouldn't listen to me. He only said curtly that it was their responsibility . . .

'I don't know what he meant by that. Actually, I wouldn't like to meet him in a dark alley, for all that he was dressed in a business suit. He looked like a brigand, and he certainly acted like one. I didn't like him; he was a bit frightening.'

Alicia noted a raised eyebrow, and more than a quirk of a smile, quickly supressed. Then those sculptured lips parted in a smile that changed the hard, austere face completely. He said, 'Oh, that would be one of our cousins—in charge of our Cairo affairs. I must tell him . . .' here the smile surfaced '. . . I must tell him to change his manner. A bit frightening, you said?' The smile widened.

Alicia couldn't believe it, the change that smile gave to this man's whole personality. But she couldn't let that affect her; she had to bring things on to her own level.

She said, 'What he might sound like to you, sick and in pain, Johnny would be different from what he would sound like to me. Of course,' she made herself look directly at what could be also another frightening man, and continued, sending her arm out in a throwaway gesture around the big luxurious room, 'this will be our affair now. I will take care of it.'

'My dear Miss Seacombe, there is nothing for you to take care of regarding your . . . manager here.' The words might be spoken in English, but they came out clipped,

Arctic-cold. 'As my cousin has already told him, everything here has been arranged and taken care of. The accident was committed by us. It belongs to us!'

'You might think it belongs to you. But it is not your
affair. It is ours. Johnny is our employee, and as such...'

'My dear Miss Seacombe,' the damned man said for
the second time, 'the matter is finished!' He went to
turn away with a hand half-raised to the patient in bed,
then abruptly swung back. 'Your...the elderly lady with
whom you travelled. She is not here?'

'No,' Alicia found herself answering without wanting
to. 'She was tired so stayed at the hotel.'

'You came here on your own...by yourself?'

'Yes.' She had only meant to say the one word, but
couldn't prevent herself from continuing as she took in
that inimical presence waiting motionless for the rest of
her answer, 'I came in a taxi.'

He, this man she was beginning to dislike more and
more, threw out both hands and spoke, and the timbre
in which the tone echoed across to her said it all. But
she couldn't take umbrage; she couldn't understand the
words. They were in Arabic. Then he was continuing in
English.

'In a common taxi? Haven't you any sense?'

'I do have sense! And if it is any of your business, it
was not a common taxi. It was a registered one the hotel
procured for me. Now, I would like to speak to...' she
had been going to say Johnny, but substituted '...my
manager.' It was as near to a dismissal as she could bring
herself to utter.

But if she had thought it a dismissal, the man dressed
in that formal white across from her certainly didn't. He
was saying, 'It was unfortunate that you decided to come
here to Egypt at all. The matter was looked after.
And...it is not at all suitable that you have. To come

to a foreign city, and an Eastern city at that...without having relations or connections to have contact with.'

'I am afraid that, unfortunate or not, I have come to Cairo. And I intend to go on to Luxor, and even further. I do have connections. With an agency, a responsible top agency, which has the care of all our stock.' She broke off as a muted exclamation came from Johnny, and, believing she knew what he was about to say, went on quickly herself.

'Also, from what I was told in Australia, all kinds of people go to this fair...to buy horses, to sell horses, and even to just look at horses.'

'Certainly. That is true. But I don't imagine there will be any women there. Their male relations or agents do any necessary trading for them.'

'Well, there's always a first time for everything,' Alicia answered a little shakily, gazing at this man, whose grimness seemed suddenly as frightening to her as that cousin Johnny had spoken of must have seemed to him. Then, as she turned, she saw him full-face for the first time, the eyes wide open. It was as if she was looking into a lake of green fire; not into an opaque jewel of deep jade, but into the bright, translucent light of a pure emerald. She seemed to be gazing right to beyond the surface. The lids had fallen, and she stood there with all thoughts of horses, of Johnny, of where she was going to go, swept from her consciousness. Motionless, silent, she remained stationary.

She heard a clipped voice say in English, 'I'll leave you then to speak with your manager. I'll see you outside.'

Unable to even make herself reply, No, don't wait. I don't want to see you again, which she knew was what she wanted to do, she turned as Johnny's familiar voice spoke to her.

So, pulling up a chair, she asked him, 'Now tell me all about it?' and listened while he did.

'It was purely an accident, Alicia,' he said. 'A man driving a desert buggy amid a herd of excited animals knocked me down, grating my leg against a brick wall. And the damned worst of it was, you know, Alicia,' he went on dismally, 'there *is* only one bloody brick building out there, and I had to be near it at that time.'

'Oh, Johnny...' Sympathy was in her voice.

However, the man lying there holding her hand was continuing, 'In some far distant past it must have been an old fort. Now it's only used to stable horses.'

'But what else is out there? Is it all desert?'

'There's a small oasis alongside of the fort which will be used by the customers when they come. Also, of course, there is the large oasis, but that's out of bounds and belongs to his people.' Johnny pointed to the door through which the man dressed in flowing white had disappeared.

'But here's the big question, Johnny? Will we sell our stock?'

'Yes—checking round out there, I think we will. Good equestrian mounts are eagerly sought after, and ours are well trained, you know. And there is Dark Shadow...' They smiled at one another.

'Is he OK? Will they look after him? You know how valuable that colt is!'

'Having met that man who has just left, and listened to him, I would think so. He is certainly something, Alicia, isn't he?'

Yes, she thought. That man who had just left was certainly something. However, even if for one quick instant a flare of attraction had seemed to pass between them, she would rather not have anything to do with him. He came from a vastly different people, a vastly different culture from the one she normally lived in and belonged to.

So she only said, after a glance at her watch, 'Johnny, I want to try and see a doctor about you before I leave...'

'He's right, you know, Alicia.' Johnny was on to something altogether different from how he was getting on. 'You can't go out to the fair. You will have to leave it all to the agency.'

'OK. I'll see,' was all she answered, unwilling to worry him. 'Now, do you need anything? Books or...'

'Oh, no. I have all the books and papers I need. And they come to see how I am all the time. You'd think I was a world-famous rock star or something. All I need, want...is to get out of here.'

'Which of course you will,' she replied, grinning at him as she had always done, then added, 'Look, I'm off now. I only hope I can find someone who can speak English.'

'No worries there. Half of them speak English.' But he wasn't thinking of the words he was saying. Hating as he did to be in here, he yet sent a rueful smile to meet hers as she flipped a hand and hurried away.

Outside, after the tiniest pause, Alicia sent slow footsteps along the corridor, to where, when they saw her emerge, a man dressed in flowing white, accompanied by another in the more ordinary hospital whites, came to meet her.

'This is Dr Raschid, Miss Seacombe,' said the Sheikh Hassan ben Amarna, and then stood back.

She found, as Johnny had said, that there was no need to worry about language. 'Mr Saunders is not my patient,' Dr Raschid said after he had greeted her. 'He is under the surgeon here, but I can tell you he is doing fine—as he should be, considering who operated on him.' Here, he glanced at the silent man across from him, then continued, 'So you need have no worries.' He smiled gently at them both and moved off down the hallway.

Alicia also shot a glance at the silent man opposite, and said, remembering her manners, 'I would like to say thank you...' and then wondered how she should address him. He stood there giving her no help whatsoever, and she felt again the dislike for him that she had done once before, but made herself carry on. 'For what your people have done for Johnny, Sheikh Hassan.' There—she only hoped she had pronounced it correctly, the emphasis on the second syllable—as she thought Johnny had done.

'It was no trouble, Miss Seacombe. I have already told you. It came about from a fault of ours. Now, shall we go?'

At least he had no servant standing behind him this time, she thought tartly, at whom to flick a finger to do his bidding, but she only said, 'I won't take up any more of your time, thank you, Sheikh Hassan. I must hurry away now or my driver might take umbrage if I am late.'

'Your driver will not take umbrage. He is not there waiting.'

'Of course he is. He will be expecting me. It is almost eight o'clock.'

'He will not be expecting you, my dear Miss Seacombe. He has gone.'

'But he can't be gone. He is a registered driver from the hotel. He must keep his appointments—if he wants to keep his job.' Alicia turned sharply away from him and moved towards the lifts.

However, the Sheikh Hassan—or whatever—kept pace with her, and spoke softly. 'He is not there because I didn't think it suitable for you to be running around a foreign city by yourself. So I am seeing you home.'

Those words did stop her hurrying footsteps. She turned, facing him, then looked quickly away from those brilliant eyes, not cool like a quiescent emerald now, but glinting like deep green water with the sun striking it. She said, 'You are not seeing me home, and I don't believe my driver would go off and leave me, just like that!'

'Oh, not just like that! Ali went down and told him to.'

'I simply don't believe you,' said Alicia for the second time. This whole scene was getting out of hand. Angry, not knowing what to make of this bizarre situation, she said breathlessly, 'You must be mad to go on like this. My driver would simply take no notice of your...your servant.'

'Oh, Ali is not my servant—well, yes, he is, but not in the manner you mean. He is a young sheikh of our people. And allow me to inform you, Miss Seacombe— and you had better believe it—that no one, *no one*, would willingly hesitate to do what a sheikh of the ben Amarna told them to do. Now, shall we go?'

'I don't care how important you are, or think you are. I am not going with you. Why, I only met you for the first time a few minutes ago...'

'Oh, surely not for the first time,' interrupted that soft English voice. 'I would say it was the second. Or, as far as I'm concerned, the third!'

Alicia gasped. She knew the colour had flown to her cheeks. They felt hot and she could actually feel them burning. He, this arrogant man, could only be referring to that look outside the airport. Which of course she had contributed to. Hadn't his image so remained in her subconscious mind that she had seen it projected in a mirror she had been using?

But now, her teeth clenched, she straightened and told him, 'Whatever it is you're saying, and I don't understand it at all, the fact remains that I hardly know you, and going with you would be much more unsuitable than going off by myself with a hotel driver. Much more un-suitable!' She moved to step nearer to the lifts.

'If you are associating me with any thoughts of a white slave trade, my dear Miss Seacombe, I beg leave to tell you that in these permissive days I hardly think it is still a flourishing business.' The voice, though it might still be speaking in English, had lost its soft drawl, only a harsh cutting edge emanating from it. 'Even if it were,' the almost frightening voice told her, 'allow me to inform you that it certainly wouldn't apply to me. If I want women—any kind of women, native-born, or modern European—I have every confidence that there would be no dearth of applicants applying to indulge me. Now, my dear Miss Seacombe, the lift is there. Shall we go?'

She could quite believe that the words he had just uttered were only too true. With that handsome coun-tenance, and having also that charisma which was an essential part of him, of course they would be. Furiously angry, knowing she was unable to answer that scathing statement, she replied to other words he had used so many times this evening. 'If you "my dear Miss Seacombe" me just once again, I will hit you, important as you are, I promise you.' She heard herself say the words, and her hand went flying to her mouth. What had possessed her? She turned sharply, stumbling swiftly to the lift, and pressed the call button.

Suddenly, the frightening, arrogant prince of this land had gone. He answered her, with amusement showing, 'I wonder that your aunt brought you up so carelessly. Physical violence indeed!'

If her cheeks had been hot before, they were on fire now. What had possessed her to say such a thing? She turned her face from him as they descended. Arriving at the ground floor, her companion kept his finger on the button to prevent the doors opening. He told her, not with a frightening harshness, nor even with that recent amusement, but with a sharp, wry astringency, 'Leaving aside the affairs which obviously fill your entire mind, I have a small, significant affair of my own to worry about. I really didn't expect to be walking through the main receiving room of the Cairo hospital tonight, dressed like this... and with you...'

'But who will see you? Visiting hours are finished, and for heaven's sake who would know you—or me for that matter?' cut in Alicia curtly.

'Will you really hit me if I say "my dear Miss Seacombe" once again? Because, believe me, I will be recognised... and this is the East... Words, affairs run like wildfire among high and low alike. My presence here, and dressed like this, which is not my usual form of attire, will be a talking point at half the breakfast tables of Cairo. Oh, well, State occasions have their formal dress—in all countries. And a State occasion is the reason for my hurry. Now, shall we walk sedately through, with you gravely discussing your manager's health with me? At least our involvement in *that* will be known throughout half of Cairo as well.'

The Sheikh Hassan's English speech stopped, and low, sharp Arabic took its place. Alicia bet herself that if she could only understand it she would hear swearing as bad as any she had overheard at home.

However, she only replied, and there was astringency in *her* voice this time, 'Sedately. Oh, yes! And I suppose we can walk straight through looking as you did at the Athens airport—as if you owned the place.'

'Oh, so you do remember the first time we met...'

God, had she always been so stupid! She answered curtly, 'We didn't meet, as you very well know. But one can't avoid noticing such behaviour.'

'All right, then. Come along now and we'll both own the place.' The lift doors slid open.

So they walked sedately through the large area, with nurses hurrying about their business; past a reception desk from which no one looked at them, to come to and pass Ali waiting at the entrance. He fell in behind her companion.

Not parked further along, as were other vehicles and taxis, the big black car stood waiting right in front of the steps, opposite a 'No Parking' sign.

Seeing it there, Alicia shook her head, but with a glance at Sheikh Hassan, who stood back, she entered the limousine as the back door was opened. He followed, and through a glass partition she saw that the driver was not clothed like an ordinary chauffeur but in the same dress as Ali, who had gone to sit beside him.

So she sat in her own corner, with the Sheikh Hassan Whatever remaining in his, and watched the fascinating city slide past.

Then, as he gave another surreptitious glance at his watch, she realised that probably all this haughty Arab prince beside her wanted to do was deposit her at the hotel and be on his way. She made herself speak. 'I really do have to go see to our horses, Sheikh Hassan. My grandfather...'

'You take umbrage when I say to you "My dear Miss Seacombe".' A hand was raised as her mouth opened to interrupt. 'However, spoken in the tone I am using now, they are the only words to convey the impossibility of you going out to that fair.'

'That is what you say!' Anger carried through her words as she replied. 'But banks, and their demands, would never worry you, I expect. However, a bank fore-closing on land we have owned for hundreds of years worries me. This situation should never have arisen but my grandfather...' Alicia stopped abruptly.

The man had turned and was actually looking at her, so Alicia made herself go on. 'I...Aunt Em and I have been trying to build a fire-break, and if our stock sells well here, we could go to the bank and say, "Go jump".'

Even if unable to understand the words echoing to her from the other side of the car, she yet understood the anger they carried. Then speech did come in a language she did understand. 'In Allah's name,' said Hassan in curt English, 'where are the men of your family?'

Alicia threw out a hand, dismissing the words. 'It doesn't matter. The only thing I am interested in is getting to see that our horses are sold for what they are worth.'

'Look——' it was not my dear Miss Seacombe with which he answered, but the tone of it was there '—it is simply out of the question for you to go. Also, Hamid's have a perfectly good auctioneer who will look after you. I don't want to discuss this any longer. I have an appointment for which I don't dare be late. So...'

'Dare! Did I hear you use that word? I wouldn't have thought you would be aware that such an expression existed.' Furiously angry at his adamant stand, Alicia didn't care what she said, and ended up with, 'And I will go to the horse fair...somehow.'

'You won't, you know!' The four words were hard, definite.

Then, unexpectedly, a soft laugh echoed across to her, and Alicia heard it with amazement. With further amazement she heard him say, amusement still echoing in his tone, 'I really am not intransigent. Why don't you relax and let things take their course for a while and see what happens? For now, if I know of the word "dare" or not, it *is* important that I am not late. Here we are.'

Thinking they had pulled up some yards from the hotel entrance, Alicia edged along the seat to follow him out. His emphatic "no" halted her in mid-stride, and she felt her foot, half in, half out, go down hard on to the unevenly gravelled shoulder of a footpath. The high heel turned under, and she was falling...

The arm which caught her tumbling body was iron-hard. She stood enclosed against him, shock holding her motionless. Then she was back to reality, to where she was . . . and how she should sharply move away. She still stood motionless! The arm around her tightened, and his head came down. The lips which came to rest upon her own were not hard, not demanding; they were moving gently back and forth—as if searching. Unconsciously, her body arched to meet his, and then the arm around her tightened yet again, spread-eagling against her back, bringing curves into hollows, her melting softness into the iron-hard body now enclosing her.

She knew what she was doing; she wasn't being wafted away. She didn't care! Her desires flew to meet those searching lips, uncaring about consequences. As if the man holding her had felt that unthinking response, she was brought even yet closer. Held hard against him, feeling those lips moving sensuously upon her own, responding completely to them, she felt as if a spring had uncoiled deep within her, silver-sharp, shining...and she was unaware of the shudder that convulsed her entire form.

The man was not unaware. His lips moved, to remain for a long second at the corner of her mouth before beginning to trail slowly, oh, so slowly downwards along a smooth, exposed throat. They paused at the opening of her blouse, to again begin that back-and-forth movement; this time upon the swelling mounds each side of it.

A small sound came from Alicia's throat. The world about her had disintegrated, everything was gone; there was only this man, those lips which were sending the soaring pulse of need, of want, into her bloodstream.

'Hell and damnation! What a time!' Alicia felt herself moved sharply away. She stood there held loosely within his encircling embrace, fair hair falling like a shining cascade of gold upon the pristine white muslin-clad arm. From somewhere far away the thought came—he spoke in English. He must have been thinking in English.

He was saying, 'I've got to go!' the strain in his voice when he had sworn and set her back changing now to harshness. He went to guide her into the car, the vehicle whose large black bulk had shielded them from both passers-by and moving traffic alike.

However, Alicia hung back, an arm outstretched entreatingly. 'I...you must know...that I don't behave...' Hassan did turn to look at her then.

'You don't imagine,' he told her sharply, 'that I myself do this sort of thing all the time? As for your behaviour—give me a little credit, Alicia, for experience gathered on my way around the world. Of course I would know if our lovemaking just now were familiar territory to you...'

'You called me Alicia...' she exclaimed, unable to preventing herself interrupting, even though she had heard his words and was thankful for them.

'Yes, I did, didn't I? That doesn't alter the fact that I simply can't waste any more time. I'll wait here while Ali escorts you. I can't risk being seen doing that if I turn up late.'

She couldn't stop herself from saying as he went to slam shut the car door, 'Will I see you again?'

For a second time the young girl saw light strike against brilliant pinpoints as a gleam of illumination caught and held those magnetic emerald eyes. He only said quickly, though she heard the amusement colouring the brisk, hurried words, 'We'll see what kismet brings, shall we?'

Then came harsh, just as hurried words in Arabic, and the limousine jumped forward. Gazing back through the window, Alicia saw that his form was already swallowed up in darkness; only a far, faint glimmer of whiteness showed that he was still there, that that scene which she had just passed through had really occurred.

In barely so few minutes they arrived at the hotel. Arriving not only there, but smack in front of the entrance. Their driver had not worried about other vehicles; had not even thought of giving right of way, she reflected astringently as she fumbled for the door handle.

However, Ali was there before her, and, stepping out, she went to say goodnight and thank you, before moving to the steps by herself. She found the man still beside her.

So she smiled again, dismissing him. 'I'm all right now, Ali, thank you. Goodnight.'

He only gestured towards the entrance, saying, 'Must hurry, lady. The lord Hassan said to see you into the hotel.'

'I'm fine now, Ali,' Alicia answered emphatically. 'Go now. The Sheikh Hassan is waiting.'

'Yes, lady, that is so. But my lord says to see you right into hotel.'

'Oh, for goodness' sake,' she was beginning, then shrugged and walked swiftly to the entrance. She went through, and received the most rapid bow possible before seeing a disappearing back clothed in colours with which she was becoming very familiar.

Glancing around the brightly lit, opulent foyer facing her, with its early evening patrons coming and going, Alicia felt she was being stared at. Still enmeshed in that intense physical experience of a passion which had sent her into a far, far different world, she wished she could pick up her swirling skirt and run. She walked sedately through both guests and the large bright surroundings while opening her small purse and beginning to rummage through it as if searching for a key. Abruptly she was being carried swiftly upwards by the lift, and was walking down a seemingly never-ending corridor—to be standing thankfully with her back against a hard, locked door.

Stepping silently across to the far bed, which had the light above it turned low, her hand went out to take up the folded nightdress. Then just as quietly she passed her sleeping aunt and was in the bathroom.

Gazing at her reflection in the bright strip lighting, she gave a gasp, horrified. No wonder she had been stared at downstairs. How stupid could she have been? She had had a compact with her; she had had a comb. It was no use telling herself that she had simply not thought of how she had looked, or thought of anything but a man's arm holding her... a man's kisses...

She drew a long sigh which seemed to come right from her toes. In two hours out of a world's lifetime, could such a cataclysmic event have overturned her existence? No, of course it hadn't, she decided, and splashed cold water across burning cheeks, over startling poppy-scarlet lips. How had she come to do such a thing? To allow... Then honesty compelled her to admit that she hadn't just allowed it; she had gone joyously to meet and respond to his every caress.

It was to that man, that Arab, to whom thanks were due that the interlude had ended as it had—not as it could have done. God! What must he be thinking of her? Probably as some trashy Western tourist out for a thrill. But... she shook her head. No, he had told her quite definitely that he would have known if that scorching, passionate love scene were familiar territory to her. Well, he had saved her some respect. His world and hers didn't come into contact. She would never have met him except for Johnny's accident and the association was now definitely finished! Hadn't he said so? She would go about—as far as she was able—the business she had come here for. She pulled the short cotton nightdress over her head, switched out the light, and, carefully making her way through the dim room, she flipped out another light and slipped into bed.

I needn't think of him, she told herself, turning her face into the pillow. I needn't think of what happened. I can look upon it as just another aberration caused by a strange land; a long flight. I can go to sleep! However, as she was slipping down into the soft darkness of oblivion, a word jumped out of her subconscious. A word she wouldn't have thought she had ever spoken. Kismet... She went over the borderland into sleep.

CHAPTER THREE

'IT'S a bit hot, isn't it?' said Aunt Em, fanning herself
with the English language newspaper she had bought.

'Oh, come on, Aunt Em.' Alicia laughed sideways at
her. 'You know you've lived in temperatures quite as hot
as this.'

'Yes, but that was at home,' replied the caustic tones
of the lady already past her three score years and ten.
Then she grinned and settled down to read her paper.

Alicia settled back too, and, flying again, she wasn't
worrying about whether she had done the wrong thing.
She knew she had! Their agents—both of them—had
left her in no doubt about that when they had arrived
at Mr Hamid's office this morning.

'Very well, I accept all you are telling us, but my niece
would like to ride Dark Shadow to show him off.' Aunt
Em could be quite as biting and condescending as that
man at the big desk before them was being; and she could
also show it just as much.

'Dark Shadow?'

'Yes, and, as your firm will get a commission, you
will want him to bring the price we expect. He has a
reserve of seventy-five thousand dollars upon him.'

Mr Hamid sat up straighter as the price reached him.
'I knew ... my man said there was a valuable colt among
your stock. However, I didn't realise ... Wait—our auctioneer is on the premises. I'll get him up.'

While they waited, Alicia asked, 'Do these people—
the ben Amarna—sell their stock at this fair?'

'Certainly they do. They are great horse breeders.'

32

'Given that,' it was Aunt Em interjecting this time, 'how is it that you say they are so powerful? Good horses do sell for large sums of money, but...'

'Yes, I am well aware of that; however, the ben Amarna have interests in many other affairs: banking and precious metals among them. It is the half-English sheikh who deals with that—in London, in Geneva... Oh, good, here is Mr Aziz.'

It was just as well his attention veered to the newcomer and to Aunt Em. Alicia felt her stomach clench as if she had suffered a blow. The half-English Sheikh! It was Hassan, she knew. That remembered so-English voice said it all.

She grinned inside herself, reflecting how like a young, insignificant female she was behaving. Because for a full minute after Mr Hamid's words she had been unable to think of anything else. Her breath had gasped from a throat gone suddenly dry. It didn't matter that Hassan was what he was. But... it suddenly made her behaviour more understandable—at least to herself.

She found the auctioneer quite happy to deal with them, and heard him say, smiling widely around at them all, 'I have rung Vienna because there is an American already here, looking for top equestrian mounts. It does no harm to have more than one interested buyer.'

No, indeed it didn't. Then, with business finished, he had walked outside to stand upon the crowded foothpath with them. He had replied quite casually to her query about helicopters, 'Yes, they go up on both the days of the sale. Maybe... I don't know—you and your Aunt may be able to get a lift.'

However, remembering a man who had informed her so unequivocally that she would not be going, Alicia asked, 'Can anyone really go? I was told that there would be no females there.'

'Well,' the big cheerful auctioneer smiled down at the young girl, 'you can always enquire.' He wasn't really interested and was turning away.

'I'm told...my manager was told,' interjected Alicia quickly, 'that I shouldn't go. Would that be correct?'

'Who was the firm or agent giving you that information. Mr Hamid?'

'No...no, it was...' She didn't want to say who it was, so only said, 'My manager heard it from some sheikh of the ben Amarna.'

The whole atmosphere around them had changed unexpectedly. She suddenly found she was not looking at a cheerful auctioneer, but at a man from an alien country. He said carefully, 'In that case, Miss Seacombe, I am afraid you will not be going. You can safely leave your valuable horses in my hands, I promise you. I will be in touch with you about reserve prices after I have seen them. Goodbye.'

Just like that he had gone, and they both stood there waiting for their taxi. 'God, I wish I were a millionaire, or the President of the US, or the Queen of England. I would show everyone here that they could do nothing to stop me going about my own business,' came wrathfully, emphatically from Alicia.

Her aunt laughed, but said with deliberation, 'Do you know, Alicia, from what I have noticed and heard about these people, these ben Amarna, if push comes to shove I don't know if you would win even then.' Disregarding her niece's frowning countenance, she had stepped complacently into the taxi pulling up beside them. So they had gone to see Johnny and were about to fly on to Luxor.

Jerked from her unhappy thoughts, Alicia opened her eyes to focus them upon the disturbance at the entrance. The last of the passengers she thought, and about time too. This plane they were in was no big jet, just a small one-class affair flying the interior. It was also not very crowded. Well, not at the front. Still, the commotion she had just heard was probably going to change all that.

Two passengers were walking the aisle to take the third seat down, and observing the colours they wore, Alicia felt for the second time that day her solar plexus clamp tight. She clasped her arms tightly about herself. After his definite leave-taking of last night, and accepting that there was no way she could get out to the desert, she hadn't expected to see either him or those colours again. Certainly not today!

She had also decided that that would be a good thing. That it had just been the excitement of being in a strange, foreign country, of almost two days of flying from one far land to another which had been the cause of her behaviour, her absolute submission to a torrid, passionate love interlude. But... honesty compelled her to acknowledge that it could also have come about by being exposed to an out-of-the-world, charismatic prince of Arabia.

The hostess was now escorting two Egyptians into the second seat, one of them wearing a burnous of familiar colours—he was not in flowing white today—who was bending solicitously down to his companion. As he straightened and turned to take his seat, the Sheikh Hassan ben Amarna's glance went around the plane. It passed over her without a flicker of recognition, and then he was seated, sandwiched in between others of his guarding escort now ensconced in the front seat.

'Good heavens,' muttered Alicia contemptuously, 'anyone would think this were the Middle Ages. Bodyguards, no less!' Glancing surreptitiously at the two Arabs in the second seat, she decided that it was probably this stranger, important from the way he was being deferred to, who could have been the reason for that urgent hurry Hassan had shown last night.

At least the newcomer wasn't in maroon and white; but his plain brown burnous was zigzagged in silver at all hemlines. Suddenly she wondered why she was even thinking of them—of him, that man of last night. Hadn't she decided in the cold practical light of day that she couldn't understand why she had behaved so? That, from what she remembered about some of that encounter, she hadn't even liked him?

So now she turned her gaze to concentrate upon the view outside the small window, and saw what could have been a thread of cotton winding through the brownness surrounding it but which was of course the great Nile river. It showed sometimes as the merest sliver of glinting silver, sometimes as a dark, sliding pewter. Then even that had gone, and only the immensity of the desert was there.

There was that shadow again. On and off, the shade of their plane had fled before them just above the sands beneath. She grinned at it, reflecting how incredibly real it appeared, this phantom plane flying exactly in the same path as their own.

Fascinated by the antics of that shadow, she turned away, startled, as the hostess said from just beside her, 'Fasten your seatbelts, please.'

And five minutes later a soft bump told her that they had arrived at Luxor—to whatever was waiting for them there.

Beginning to rise as a bustle sounded from the seats behind them, they were motioned back by the hostess who had come to block the aisle just ahead of them.

Oh, of course, thought Alicia tartly—their important passengers had to be allowed an unimpeded exit. At least all this pomp and show explained why she wasn't even on the periphery of the Sheikh Hassan's world. Last night had most probably been just an aberation for him too.

With Aunt Em's arm through hers, they eventually walked across the wide open ground to the small white administration centre. There, too, the other passengers were held back, and Alicia saw a troop of horses waiting. Dressed in their loosely flowing burnous, straight-backed on beautiful, splendid animals, the riders looked fierce, wild.

Standing in the front row watching, Alicia wasn't for the moment looking at the riders; she was assessing the horses. Then with a flurry of movement their erstwhile plane passengers were mounting. Stepping into a stirrup being held for him, Hassan went into the saddle like a dancer, every muscle, every action a poem of fluid movement.

Abruptly, however, the watching girl thought—he couldn't have! He couldn't have fumbled a lost rein. Not that rider! But the beautiful Arab horse had swung round to pass almost on top of them, and, leaning from the saddle as if clutching for a strap, the rider's head was near, and words coming to her also from so near were saying, 'Now, about that matter of Kismet...'

Only she could have heard them. Not being frightened of horses, she had not edged back. But now, in swift strides, both rider and mount were at the head of the troop, and in silence, in exact precision, they had gone, cantering swiftly away as if in formation.

Lying back in her corner of the taxi taking them on the long journey into Luxor, driving through a jungle of green hemming in both sides, Alicia only replied absently to her Aunt's comments, her thoughts completely upon six words which had reached out to her from low on a horse's flank. Kismet! He had said that last night, at the very last. Did he mean...? Did he intend to see her again? They had been a laughing six words, she was almost sure.

Damn him, she reflected. This morning she had sent both him and that torrid interlude of last night into the furthermost recesses of a mind determined to banish them. However, remembering still the arrogant way he had countermanded her wishes, that was where she intended to keep him. There might be some sort of interaction she acknowledged; however, when it came down to it, she didn't really like him.

Abruptly she sat up straight, other thoughts wiped from her consciousness. Before their moving vehicle three immense palms rose to the heavens, and between their lacy spread of fronds a slice of infinity was caught, held there in a colour of indigo mixed with lapis lazuli so intense, so breathtaking that she strove to hold it to her. Then they were past and it was gone, and a caustic voice from beside her said, 'Here we are!'

Yes, there they were, pulling in to park before the usual high-rise tourist hotel. 'This is the new Winter Palace,' said their driver proudly as he carried their baggage in.

'The new Winter Palace?' asked Alicia.

'Yes, the old one we had isn't big enough now, so we built a new one,' said their guide cheerfully.

Upstairs, gazing out of the big glass window, Alicia looked down at the Nile as she had done in Cairo, at the palm-clustered embankment guarding it as it slid past on its way. She flung herself down on the bed and asked, 'What now, Aunt Em?'

'Look Alicia, forget about Dark Shadow and enjoy yourself in this new country you have read so much about. These people—these ben Amarnas will look after things, I'm sure. And Dark Shadow is lovely, and will sell on his own merits. You'll see.'

'Yes, I suppose so, but if only Johnny had been there.' While saying those words, of course her thoughts went to the reason why he wasn't—and also to the reason she wasn't going out there to take his place. Because an arrogant, overbearing man had said no. In any proper civilised country, of course she would have been able to go, went her thoughts wrathfully.

Then, seeing the worried look her aunt was bending upon her, she smiled that radiant smile that only surfaced so occasionally, and said, 'Sorry, love. Now tell me what you would like to do?'

'Go for a walk, I think. I feel I have been sitting down for a week or more. Also we might pick up some brochures from the desk.'

They did pick up some brochures, then went across to stroll along the river, walking slowly under the dark ebony shadow of palm trees one moment, then into the bright sunshine of early evening the next.

'Oh, look, there's a Light and Sound spectacular on at the Karnak temple tonight,' said Alicia.

'And also just look—something I didn't expect. Here is a notice enquiring for a bridge player,' said her Aunt Em, reading from her pile of brochures. 'That will do me. Now, what about you, Alicia.'

'I'll ring Johnny, then go up to bed after an early dinner. Jet lag is beginning to catch up with me, I think. You go and slay them at bridge, darling Aunt Em, and I'll enjoy myself at the Valley of the Kings tomorrow.' So, with a last, lingering glance over this famous waterway, they returned to what their guide had proudly told them was the new Winter Palace.

Then, as they walked through the foyer, an American voice hailed them, 'Hi there, you two,' and they were being abruptly surrounded by the archaeology group. 'We've come to pick up Charles, who is here on business,' Sally told them, laughing. 'We're taking him to Karnak as he's only here for two nights and is off the next day. Are you going, Alicia?'

'No, I have some phoning to do. Perhaps another time?' What else could she say? She wasn't going to this magic place on her own, even if that had been practical. However, she did gaze a little wistfully after the moving, happy group with the man she had just been introduced to walking in its centre. She still watched as they made their way carelessly, confidently through the big foyer, to disappear in an excited, laughing unit, then she turned and followed her aunt.

Upstairs, hanging out a skirt she had just unpacked from her case, she turned, arrested, as a knock came upon their door. 'Who could that be, Aunt Em?' she wondered. 'The hotel would use the telephone.'

'You can always find out by answering it,' said her aunt in her most caustic tone.

'Yes, I expect so,' replied Alicia, and she was laughing over her shoulder at the older woman as she went to do just that.

She glanced at the man standing there and remained perfectly motionless, silent. Unexpected shock kept her so.

'My lord Hassan sends you this,' said Ali.

Alicia found that for the space of a long heartbeat she could not reach out to accept the proffered letter, then, taking the deep necessary breath, she said, 'Thank you,' and held out her hand.

She noticed fleetingly the scroll of Arabic lettering across the top of the heavy cream envelope, and then, as normality returned, saw that it was addressed to Miss Alicia Seacombe in a slashing black hand. She went to close the door and take it inside, thinking somewhere far back in a mind still not entirely with it that at least it wasn't addressed to, 'My dear Miss Seacombe.'

Ali's hand went out to prevent the door closing. He said, 'My lord says to take back an answer.'

Gazing down at the dark, sprawling, unfamiliar writing, Alicia slowly turned the envelope over. Carefully she endeavoured to unseal the flap without tearing it, but suddenly, glancing sideways, saw that Ali was watching her. Angry somehow, she simply tore open the envelope and withdrew a single sheet of the heavy ivory paper, folded over once.

The same dark writing which had addressed the outer covering said without preamble...

There is a Light and Sound on at Karnak tonight. I thought that as a young romantic tourist you might like to see it; maybe to compensate for your not going out into the desert. I will pick you up at seven.

It was not even signed. Probably because he didn't know which title to assume, thought Alicia astringently. It was not even addressed either, and he did know which title to call *her* by. She would simply have loved to say, 'Tell your lord Hassan that I am already engaged.' But knew she wouldn't—even if she had been. She said instead, 'Thank you, Ali. I will be ready.'

She stood at the open door watching him walk down the long corridor. She also watched a large party of guests emerging from the lift part before him as he went on his way regardless. She decided with a shake of her head that it wasn't even deliberate. That he went his way as he was accustomed to do. She went inside.

Handing the torn envelope and letter to her aunt, she said a little breathlessly, 'It seems I am to go out also tonight,' and waited while those wise old eyes perused the few lines.

'I expect it is meant for you,' said the caustic voice, 'although it has no salutation to head it, nor signature to end it.'

'It is from the Sheikh Hassan ben Amarna. I told you about him. He was with Johnny when I went to the hospital. He brought me home. I told you!'

'Yes, you did tell me! But this note says there is more to it than that! Look, Alicia, you know I never in-

terfere... but this country is different from the one you
normally live in. That fact applies to this man also. He
could be dangerous...'

'He is not interested in me if that is what you mean.
Considering who he is and what he looks like, he could
most likely have any woman with the merest inclination
of his head. He is just being kind because of Johnny's
accident.'

'Alicia, really... I would expect there are other ways
for men to show their desire to be helpful. Very well,
but remember Kipling's saying...'

'I know what Kipling said. However, that was a long
time ago. Things are changing now. Anyway, Hassan is
as much English as he is Arab.' Alicia didn't know what
had made her say that. She didn't even believe it was
true. God, hadn't he shown her what an Arab thought
of her going alone among patrons of a horse-fair?

Her aunt's shoulders went up. 'At least,' she said, 'I
know where I am when I am playing bridge, I can always
pull out if the bidding gets too high. You see that you
are able to do the same, Alicia.' Aunt Em went into the
bathroom.

Alicia collapsed into a huddle of laughter. Good
heavens—if the bidding got too high! It wasn't she who
had pulled out last night, it was Hassan! But tonight he
was only taking her to see a famous tourist attraction.
He had said so in his note, hadn't he?

CHAPTER FOUR

COMPACT, comb, tissues, and of course money—even if she didn't expect to use it—went into the small evening bag. Alicia gave a last look at herself in the mirror.

The skirt she had finally picked out, softly yellow, was mid-calf; the blouse had a deeply smocked scooped-out neckline, and was one she had bought at Athens airport. Eye-lined and shaded, blue eyes she had forbidden to sparkle returned her serious gaze. And for a reason she wouldn't acknowledge she had outlined her lips more heavily than usual in the deep fuchsia pink she had also worn at the airport. Yes, she looked like a young girl going on a date.

She heard the knock—not a hard, decisive one, just ordinary—and, picking up her bag, went carefully to open the door. For the second time that day she stood motionless within the opening, gazing at the waiting figure.

It didn't register, the form, the figure standing there. The deep lake of emerald-green fire she was looking into did. With the light behind her shining fully upon his face, she was gazing unexpectedly into wide-open eyes.

He was speaking, but for a moment she didn't hear him, and then she did. He was saying, 'Good evening, Alicia,' then, with no answer forthcoming, a black eyebrow went high.

Her breast rose and fell as she took in a deep breath. She said a little breathlessly, 'I didn't expect you.'

If that eyebrow could be said to raise any higher, it did, and his voice, which had been soft, pleasant, went curt. 'You were expecting someone else? My apologies if I have been mistaken. I had supposed...'

Breaking into those antagonistic, haughty words, Alicia spoke hurriedly. 'No, I'm sorry... I had expected Ali...'

In her turn she was interrupted, 'Ali...in the name of God why? Would I send a servant to call for a friend I was taking out?'

She registered the word 'friend', but she had other things to think of: that an outing to which she had so looked forward had now started off so disastrously. 'I only meant...' she stammered, 'that I didn't know if you...' God, she couldn't say 'didn't want to be seen with me'.

The other dark eyebrow climbed to join the first, but that frightening tone had departed. 'Look,' said the Sheikh Hassan ben Amarna, 'shall we begin again? Good evening, Alicia.'

Yes, she thought, you can begin again, but do I say, Good evening, Hassan? She did say it, and saw suddenly for the briefest second a running gleam of emerald fire, as if amusement had lit up those eyes. However, if there was a shadow of laughter colouring the soft voice, it disappeared when he told her, 'There, that is better. Shall we go?'

As he spoke, the man reached out a hand to pull shut the door. He turned then to smile down at her as she fell in beside him. It was an ordinary, pleasant smile, with no sign of the arrogance or frightening haughtiness previously displayed.

He said, 'Is your aunt having dinner before she goes to play bridge?' His question was only absent, just an enquiry to make conversation.

Alicia stopped abruptly. 'How did you know Aunt Em was to play bridge?' she asked, puzzled.

'I know! Does it matter?' This time his words were again curt.

'But you couldn't have. It was only arranged an hour or so ago.'

'Allow me some manners, Alicia. Of course I knew! I would not have sent you this invitation if I hadn't known your aunt was otherwise engaged.'

She didn't understand it, and looked up at him. He put the lightest of fingertips upon her elbow, saying, 'If you don't begin walking, you are going to miss the start of the Karnak show. Just take it that I did know, Alicia, and forget it.'

Those words did start her walking. And the tone in which they were uttered did make her drop the subject, but she said, 'Very well, but you are not omniscient, even if you ben Amarna act as if you were.'

Unexpectedly, his eyes lit with laughter, and he told her, 'No, we might not be, but my uncle thinks we are.'

They joined a couple waiting for the lift, and Hassan gave them a polite, soft good evening, which was returned. The man dressed in a dinner suit, raised an eyebrow at Hassan, and, receiving the word, 'Foyer,' pressed the button. From where she was standing between the wall and her escort, Alicia saw the woman, also dressed for an evening out dining, beautifully groomed, perfectly made-up, allow an assessing glance to rove carefully, discreetly over Hassan. It moved slowly upwards to stop at his face, and the younger girl recognised the expression that look contained.

Mentally she shrugged. That was how she herself would view this man, if she had seen him for the first time as he was now. Outstandingly handsome, fatally attractive in a sensual way, dressed not in a dinner suit but in tight cream linen trousers and a cream long-sleeved silk shirt opened three buttons down from a tieless collar. It wasn't fair, she thought, seeing how that outfit ex-

posed the strong brown throat rising from it, the lightness
of its colour giving an added bronze tinge to his skin.
Oh, yes, she could understand that look.

Out of the lift and into the foyer, she walked its length
beside him, no fingertips on her arm this time. And
encountered glances that rested casually upon them, but
then returned for a not so casual one. She also noticed
that none of the three clerks at the reception desk were
among those who looked. Of course, he belongs to the
ben Amarna, thought Alicia tartly.

The big black limousine was not parked at the kerb
before the hotel, as it had been before the hospital entrance, but directly across on the embankment. There
was a figure lounging against the bonnet who straightened as they appeared, and moved to open the back door.
Ali ushered them in, then went round to slip in beside
the chauffeur.

Words were spoken sharply in Arabic from beside her,
and the answer coming from the front seat was certainly
not as sharp, yet it held determination. Hassan spoke
again, and Alicia knew that he was cross. Leaning over,
he pressed a button and an opaque glass partition rose.
He pressed another one and the two side windows went
down, allowing the outside world to surround them.

'You were angry about something, Hassan?' she
asserted.

However, her companion only laughed. 'I suppose,'
he said, 'I expected this to be just a private date, but I
should have known better.'

'It is a private date, isn't it?'

'As far as it will ever be with me, here in Egypt, I
expect,' she was answered. Then Hassan laughed and
told her, 'I did have some idea of taking you to the temple
in a horse-drawn carriage, but I am afraid...'

'Did you really, Hassan? I would have loved that,' she
said, and smiled widely across at him before turning to

look out as the slow-moving limousine passed not one but two of the horse-drawn carriages.

'Still,' she went on, 'I love this just as much. All elegance and luxury. Do you always drive in these sorts of cars, Hassan? You had one in Cairo too.'

'Yes we did, didn't we?' said a soft voice, and he was suddenly laughing down at her. Seeing his face, so close, Alicia remembered what had happened standing protected by that same car. She felt the hot colour run across her cheeks and throat, staining them a deep crimson. She went to move away from him, but her hand was caught and her fingers entwined between other hard fingers. She gazed down at the clasped hands laced together on the seat between them and felt the *frisson* of tension which ran through her whole body.

As if the man had felt it also, he said, 'Look, we are going to see and hear this Karnak thing, and I expect you to give it all your attention, because you have no idea of all the stratagems and deviousness I have had to resort to to get this one night to myself.'

'Should you really be doing something else, Hassan? Was it important?' she was asking, but turned to glance sideways as a hail echoed across to them. They were passing the American contingent crowded into one small horse-drawn carriage. They had seen her and were waving. Alicia waved back and then their vehicle was past.

'Are they friends of yours?' enquired a voice which held a strange nuance within it.

'Not really. I only met them while we were waiting for the plane in Athens. And the man on this side just now at the hotel.'

'Yes, I saw.'

'I think I told you once before that I don't know how you could have seen anyone . . . or anything. Your glance seemed to pass over empty space.'

Hassan only laughed, and moved to settle himself more comfortably.

Alicia tried to keep her hand perfectly still in that entwined embrace. She might not altogether like him—she certainly didn't trust him—but she didn't want those warm fingers to unclasp from hers.

Her thoughts were broken into. 'Here we are,' said her companion.

The limousine had pulled into a large open-air car park, driving, however, away from tourist coaches, cars and carriages, to come to a halt on a far side. Their door was opened and, stepping out, Hassan leaned in to help her alight. Alicia looked, bemused at the mighty bulk of the temple rising beyond this busy place where ankle-length-robed natives talked and laughed, apparently not interested at all in this vast edifice that their long-ago ancestors had built.

Alicia wondered suddenly with a little shiver if the shades of those long departed inhabitants still occupied this place.

'Are you all right?' Hassan must have seen that involuntary ripple of muscles because he looked down at her, puzzled.

And abruptly, without knowing why, she moved closer to him, wanting to feel the security of his solid body—anyone's solid body. She told him, half laughing, half seriously, 'Yes, I'm fine. I just wondered for a moment if any spirits of the people who built and worshipped here were reluctant to leave it.'

Suddenly, all was normal again and Hassan was laughing down at her, his shoulders shaking. 'Shame on you, Alicia,' he exclaimed. 'And you possessing not one drop of blood belonging to the mystic East. Now, I've played among its sands and tumbled stones all through my childhood. I have even taken a guest through this

Light and Sound thing, and no spirits have ever haunted me! Now come along.'

She went along, walking through a double row of statues which guarded the entrance, while hearing as they went the story of the building of this temple. Alicia listened, entranced. There was no visible loudspeaker, but that beautifully trained English voice echoed all around, everywhere. Then, as darkness suddenly surrounded them, her arm was caught and she was pulled close. She went against the hard, solid body thankfully, because that voice was telling them of frightening things.

Then just as suddenly they were bathed in brilliance, and, expecting to be freed, Alicia looked up on finding she was still being firmly held. Hassan was regarding her with what was almost a lopsided grin. He said, 'There are a great many people here, I might lose you.'

For the second time that night, the colour of scarlet washed her cheeks, and she turned quickly to look where she should have been looking—at a vast column that rose to the very sky. She trailed her fingers along the rough sandstone, and turned impulsively to utter an enquiry—but was pre-empted. 'Don't even begin to ask as I know you are going to,' said her companion. 'Of course I accept that the building of this place was a triumph of some master mind, but—I also think the money and the toil could have been spent on better things.'

'Do you really, Hassan? But men have built memorials since time began—even if a different sentiment was behind each one. I just think you are a Philistine not to appreciate this vast, soaring edifice built to some God someone worshipped. It awes me.'

'Well, it doesn't awe me! I am not a romantic like you, I am afraid. I am a modern man of today's world, in which I find I have to live today, and of which I have to accept the customs...and the laws——' The last remark was cut short as that wonderful beckoning voice encouraged them towards a grandstand which had certainly been built by no ancient hand. Alicia found she was sitting on a broad plank of wood with Hassan squeezed in tightly by her side, their two bodyguards immediately behind. She felt the length of his hard thigh against her own as he moved, his body brushing her own body as the crowd turned first one way and then the other.

'Look,' the whisper came from the face so close, so she did as she was bid, and saw the light pinpointing the statue of a woman standing tall, beautiful as if alive, not carved from some unyielding stone. 'And look,' said Hassan again.

Alicia's gaze followed his pointing finger. Away in the desert, a long way away, the faintest of light was becoming visible, turning from the palest green to a pulsating emerald. Out of nowhere an oasis was forming, date-palms etching their fronds against a night sky. 'Oh, it's beautiful,' she murmured.

'How is it done?' she asked, her entire interest on that incredible appearance of a living oasis, and, not even thinking, she put out her hand to rest upon the thigh lying closely alongside her own. She went to pull it away as if burnt by open fire, but hard brown fingers fastened tightly and kept it there.

That seductive voice was coming to the end of its story, and beside her Hassan slid down from the grandstand and, raising hands to clasp her waist, swung her down also. 'I don't really want to get caught in this crowd for an hour or so on the way out,' he told her, 'so we'll leave now.' They went, bypassing the temple proper, she noticed, and picked their way through large tumbled stones.

'Did I inform you that you were having dinner with me tonight, Alicia?' asked Hassan as he walked carefully along with a hand holding her elbow, one guard going before, one after.

'No, I don't remember you telling me that. I can't remember dinner being mentioned at all. But then maybe in the thrill of going to see Karnak I could have allowed words to slip by me.'

'Oh, that being the case, then, did you not hear me inform you that you will be having it at my home?'

'No, I don't remember you telling me that either!'

'So now you know, are you going to accept?'

'Yes, please.' Alicia skirted a large piece of granite barring her way as she spoke the two words.

She turned sharply as she felt the big body so close, shaking. He was laughing, his entire form quivering.

'At my home, Alicia, and you answer with two words, just like that! Shouldn't it be I, the wicked sheikh, urging you into my parlour, and you, the shrinking maiden trying desperately to find a way out? Yes please, indeed! It is certainly a changing world.'

'It is a little different, though, Hassan, for when I look at you I don't see a large villain with a big drooping moustache looming over me. I see you! Also...you could have behaved so differently last night. You know you could have...' Alicia hesitated, and her face now was not coloured a brilliant scarlet. It was pale.

'Last night was last night, and so whatever I wanted to do—and believe me, I did want to carry on—I couldn't. Because I had an appointment for which I dared not be late...'

'I can't associate you with the word "dare", Hassan,' Alicia couldn't prevent herself interrupting.

'Oh, yes, I can manage to manipulate most things, but certainly not one concerning a state dinner and conference...' Hassan stopped speaking as they arrived at the limousine into which Ali ushered them. He then continued on as if there had been no interruption, 'I can usually manage, and I have managed to get a whole twenty-four hours to myself, so we can enjoy a pleasant, leisurely dinner and evening.

'I will only add that there will be no recurrence of that interlude which happened on the way home from the hospital. I certainly didn't want it to happen then! It came right out of the blue! Nothing will come out of the blue like that tonight.' He hesitated, before continuing. 'I will also inform you that I didn't like it. I have never found before that I couldn't control everything... everything that concerned me.'

Alicia sat looking straight before her. What could she answer? That that interlude had come out of the blue for her as well; that she had never indulged in that sort of lovemaking?

As if the man had sensed some of her thoughts, he glanced down, and a long brown finger went under her chin to turn her face towards him. 'Make a pact with me, Alicia,' he said. 'Just treat tonight as a night out of time. Don't think of your horses. Don't think of your country—or mine. Only come with me and enjoy yourself. Because I am going to. I've scrounged twenty-four hours and I am going to enjoy every one of them and let the following ones take care of themselves.'

What did he mean? She felt shaken, but there was also another sensation churning beneath the flat span of her midriff. Then she admonished herself. I am not going happily into those hours yawning before me as I would do if this man were different, for I know that he is not. Still, I am going! Even if given the choice now this minute, and the car stopped, I would go!

'Here we are,' came words to interrupt her thoughts. She saw that they had driven through the long boulevard between the hotels and the river embankment and were now among buildings. They had stopped before a high blank wall.

'Dare I say, come into my parlour, my dear Miss Seacombe?' Alicia glanced up at him. She had been warned—at home, here in Egypt, and by her aunt. She laughed gaily up at him, and curtsied, saying, 'Thank you, my lord Hassan. I'd be delighted.'

He shook his dark head, indicating that she go before him as the big heavy gate opened. He said, 'Very well, but I give warning now. Maybe I might rescind some of those things I said in the car just now. Perhaps I will hold us both responsible for anything that might happen in these coming hours.'

Again came that churning of fluttering butterfly wings deep inside her. But she trod deliberately inside, and watched the bearded gatekeeper shut and bolt the door behind them then walk off along a side path, the familiar coloured burnous swirling about him.

It was no *Arabian Nights* palace into which she stepped. It did have smooth lawns and flowerbeds and the ubiquitous palms, and from somewhere a night-blooming flower wafted its perfume to the air all about them.

A few steps ahead of her Hassan was swinging open a wrought-iron gate set in another high blank wall. The room into which she walked beside him was also not from an *Arabian Nights* fantasy, but the tiles on which she found herself stepping could have been. They gleamed up at her, intricately patterned in the so many different shades of lapis lazuli. The only windows were high up along a far wall, scrolled wrought-iron enclosing them.

Her gaze went further, to a small round dining-table set for dinner, and there across from it a large, wide couch with cushions scattered carelessly on it. Their colours matched the floor and went running, glinting to meet the light.

Into the silence encircling their two immobile forms, his words reached out to her. 'Dare I tell you, Alicia, that this place was once upon a time the harem quarters?'

She met the brilliant smile he was bending upon her, the flame of emerald from eyes wide open for a change. 'Once upon a time?'

He was laughing across at her. 'Yes—this place is now my father's home, and these are now my quarters.'

'Even if they are your quarters, they could, I expect, be used for their original purpose!'

Her hand went flying to her mouth as if to hold back the words. What had possessed her to say them? She had known this tall, self-assured, arrogant and handsome man for only two days, and she had said that to him. What *had* possessed her? It would serve her right...

Interrupting, he told her—and his eyes weren't laughing now; hoods had fallen over them to allow only the merest slits to be seen—'I think maybe you had better powder your nose. Mustapha will be serving dinner in five minutes.'

He indicated a door, closed it behind her. Alicia saw two yawning archways, through one of which the gleam of brilliant tiles showed. She went through to it; the bedroom with its wide opening she ignored.

She washed her hands, powdered her nose as she had been told, combed the flyaway hair into place. She used a heavier hand than normally with the fuchsia lipstick.

She went back inside.

Her escort to Karnak was speaking with another man beside the laid table. Dressed in only a long white jibbah, he turned as Hassan did to watch as she stood immobile at the edge of the big room. Hassan didn't put out a hand to welcome her, so she made herself walk, one foot after another, across the brilliant polished tiles to meet them. He just said, 'This is Mustapha, my friend and companion for many years.'

She gazed at this newcomer on the periphery of her expanding world, this acknowledged friend, wondering what to say, how to address him. Ten years or so older than the owner of this place, this one-time harem, she surmised, but not at all like him. He said gravely, 'I'm happy to meet you, Miss Seacombe,' in English, even if in accented English.

The iron grip which had seemingly held her fast cracked a little, and she replied, sending all her considerable charm into the greeting, 'I am happy to meet you also, Mustapha,' and saw his hand go up palm outward as he turned to leave.

The charm, the smile departed when she turned to glance at the other man. He must have seen the look in her eyes, because *his* hand went up in the same gesture. He only said, however, 'You take risks, Alicia—at a time and in a place where you really shouldn't. Because you are absolutely right. This place could be used for the purpose it was originally created for. *Quite* easily, if you take my feelings into consideration.'

She heard the words; she knew what they could mean, and also how she herself had contributed to such an exchange earlier. But the man must have looked at her more closely, for he said, an eyebrow going high, 'Really, Alicia, don't look so unhappy. Be my guest for a dinner which I hope will be a pleasant one.'

He took hold of her hand and then, so unexpectedly, raised the fingertips to his lips—for all the world like a seventeenth-century gallant. Alicia felt the jolt of jumping pulses and without volition, without premeditation, she sank down in a curtsy, not laughingly as she had done before outside, but deep down as she had been taught to do at her débutante ball.

'Thank you, my lord Hassan,' she told him. 'I will endeavour to make it so.'

He smiled at her as he raised her up, a charming, captivating smile, and for a second time she felt the thud of a heartbeat changing. But Hassan only pulled out a chair for her, saw that she was seated before moving round to his own chair. 'Now,' he said, 'You can tell me the story of your life while we eat.'

'Oh, no, I can't,' she was beginning, but fell silent as Mustapha set a plate before her.

'Very well, but you can eat,' said her companion when she made no attempt to do so, and picked up his own fork to begin.

Yes, she probably could, she thought—if she could forget...if she didn't remember a smile which had abruptly set a new dimension to an already uneasy relationship. She brought a sliver of what was on her plate to her mouth. She glanced up into a watching face.

'Do you like it?' asked her companion.

'As it's delicious, you would know I do. It's some sort of fish, isn't it? I don't think I've ever tasted it before, and I most certainly haven't experienced that unusual tang running through the sauce. What——?'

'Don't begin to ask,' said a voice she had heard say the same words at Karnak, then continued on, 'I never ask. Food is just something set before me at mealtimes.'

'If it is this kind of food set before you all the time, you wouldn't need to ask,' replied Alicia somewhat astringently. 'I don't suppose you have even boiled an egg for yourself.'

Suddenly the handsome, charismatic face was laughing. 'Do you know,' he told her when the laugh had turned into only a smile, 'I believe I never have. However, if I found I had to I expect I could. In my work I do much more hazardous things...'

'You work...? What is your work, Hassan?'

She was not answered. Mustapha was changing plates. He was also filling fluted glasses from a jug with beads of moisture running down its silver sides. Alicia gazed down at what looked like baby chickens or tiny birds set in a sea of raspberry sauce. She didn't know if she wanted to eat them.

'What are they...?' She was beginning as Mustapha left the room.

A hand was raised to her palm outwards. 'Don't begin...'

'To ask...' finished Alicia.

'Eat your salad and then try them,' she was ordered. So she picked up her fork.

'About the word "work" which you just mentioned, Alicia. Did *you* work at home?'

'Not at a job as such, but I worked on the property,' answered Alicia, taking up a forkful of salad.

'You mentioned money worries. Will they be over when you sell these horses?'

'You said when, Hassan. Isn't it an an "if"?'

'Oh, I don't think that will be the case,' replied a confident voice. 'They will sell, I expect.'

Alicia looked up suspiciously. 'I don't want... You can't make people buy horses. Even you!' She told him.

'My dear...' His words were cut off as her hand was raised palm outwards. But he continued on, 'Look, I don't want to talk about your horses. Tell me about your life.'

'My life *was* horses. We raised them. We sold them. And I rode them in equestrian events. My life was quite mundane. I'll bet that doesn't apply to you.'

Ignoring her last words, he said, 'Surely it was not all work? What about friends... boyfriends?'

These words did make her look directly across at him. She said, a trifle tartly, 'Seeing that I am reasonably attractive...'

'Oh, yes, I'll drink to that.' The soft words reached across to her.

She knew that a tide of pink had come to colour her cheeks, and told him, her tone even sharper, 'So of course I had partners . . . to dances, to picnics, to affairs in Brisbane during the Exhibition . . .'

'Exhibition?'

'It's a display put on every year of all the things we have and do.'

'Oh, I know of those affairs from Europe. Social events are a part of them, aren't they. Surely you had special men to escort you around? What about that man in hospital, the one you call Johnny?'

What business was it of his what she did or didn't do? Tonight, as he had told her, was a night out of time. She would leave Egypt in two or three days and never see him again. So why dwell on her past life? She said astringently, even a little angrily, 'No, no special men. But I'm sure the same could not be said of you.'

'Oh, yes, it could! Not *no* girlfriends, but certainly no special one.'

Across a table laden with gleaming silver and crystal they looked at one another, the tall, handsome man, eyes shining like a glittering lake of emerald, hidden suddenly as falling lids hooded them; and a young girl with apricot skin giving to eyes a deeper shade of blue, with fair hair cascading in a running shimmer of light to her shoulders. Between them stretched an invisible cord of threaded steel, strong, seemingly unbreakable.

Mustapha entered on silent feet. He said in his accented English while he was refilling Alicia's almost empty glass, 'Will you have coffee here with your dessert, my lord, or——?'

'Yes,' interrupted Hassan, 'we'll have it here at the table. Tell Mustapha how you like your coffee, Alicia.'

Hesitating for a fraction of a second, she then said, 'I don't like coffee very much—except for the occasional cappuccino. So thank you, Mustapha, I'll just finish my fruit juice.'

'Yes, of course,' came the reply in English. Then Hassan was speaking in quick Arabic to him. He nodded and went away.

Alicia picked up her glass. The delicious liquid it contained she was not familiar with, but it certainly contained no alcohol. She gazed at the one beside her companion's plate, and as she did so saw his eyes dancing, wicked with amusement, laughing at her.

'You don't know what I was going to ask!' Indignation showed through her words.

'I knew!'

Angrily she wished she could wipe that superior expression off his face. She knew by his attitude, his overwhelming amusement, that he *had* known what she had been about to ask. But then, she admonished herself, there had been no need to enquire. Of course he was a Muslim. Of course he didn't drink alcohol. She looked away and began to nibble at a pastry Mustapha had set before her.

Without volition her glance went to the two long-fingered bronzed hands lying there, one of which had pushed aside his plate of dessert, untouched, the other loosely holding the stem of his glass. Of course, even if... of course there would be no sign of a ring mark. She didn't know if Muslims even wore wedding-bands. Hassan wore no rings of any sort.

Mustapha was once again by her side. He had set a cup of dark black coffee beside his master. However, glancing down at the cup set beside her, Alicia saw a swathe of thick foaming milk. She smiled up at him, saying thank you. She looked at the other man and didn't speak at all. She picked up the small silver coffee spoon and stirred the cream each way until it dissolved somewhat, then raised her cup.

CHAPTER FIVE

TAKING an experimental sip, Alicia half smiled, thinking she liked it. It tasted like no coffee she had drunk before, including Irish coffee. Abruptly, with that thought surfacing, she took a larger sip and, swallowing it, set down the cup. She looked across at that handsome, assured face gazing blandly back at her.

Should she mention it? Did he mean her to? Of course he did! This was deliberate.

'Is your coffee plain black, or does it have additives like mine?' she asked carefully.

Hassan laughed across at her, and unexpectedly she saw not hauteur, not hard arrogance, but a kind of happiness in that classically handsome face. He said, without answering her question, 'Drink your coffee and then we'll go and sit over there on that couch. We have things to talk about and I have an invitation for you.'

Unexpectedly, completely out of the blue, circumstances between them changed. She might still be a little apprehensive of him, remembering how ruthless he could be, how arrogantly he took only his own desires into consideration; but she took in that happy look and sloughed off those impressions, sending a smile across to him. A radiant smile so seldomly used.

She didn't notice the hand about his glass clench tight as he saw that smile, but she did hear him say quite harshly, 'A nice friendly chat, Alicia! Not at all one that that smile could bring into being. But one ending with an invitation I expect you will be quite pleased to accept.' He paused for a moment, then added, with his voice unexpectedly carrying the previous harshness, 'Now finish your coffee! Whatever it contains, it is not the prelude to a rape scene, alcohol-induced or otherwise, I promise you.'

'Promises, promises...' Startled by the words issuing, she opened her eyes wide in astonishment. What had possessed her? This man was not some ordinary country youth with whom she was used to bandying witticisms. And that was the second time...

However, Hassan was only laughing. His face, his voice held an altogether different expression as he explained, 'Oh, if seduction were on my mind, it would have taken a different turn from this, and be also in a very different place from this, I promise you!' His hand went out in a throwaway gesture to the large, charming room about them.

'Finished?' he asked as she set down her cup, and at Alicia's nod pushed back his chair. He settled her upon the wide couch, heaping cushions behind her back. She kept her attention away from the large, assured body so close, so very close... but couldn't prevent herself from becoming aware of an aftershave blending in with the night-flowering fragrance which had wafted about them all evening. She watched Mustapha clearing away silver and crystal and, when finished, go away, closing the door softly behind him.

Hassan took hold of her hand, playing with her fingers.

Alicia looked down upon them, remembering how they had lain entwined on the seat of the limousine going to Karnak. He was saying slowly as if searching for words, 'I mentioned before about a time-slot of twenty-four hours. I am leaving Luxor at five o'clock tomorrow, Alicia.'

Not understanding his words, she felt as if she had stepped into a lift which had shifted beneath her feet.

How stupid of her to think that, she thought. She had never expected anything would come of meeting this man, this so obnoxious, haughty yet nevertheless charismatic man. One, moreover, who walked in such a different strata from the one she herself inhabited.

She still couldn't prevent herself saying, 'Leaving Luxor!'

'Yes, a helicopter will be waiting to take me off then.'

'You are leaving Egypt?'

'No, I am not leaving the country. I am, however, going out into the far desert. Taking some officials there.'

'Oh . . . ! I too will be leaving here in two days.'

'Yes, but you will be going home with your horses sold. You should be happy about that. It is what you came here for!'

There was nothing she could answer to that. It was patently true. She couldn't prevent herself saying, however, 'Still, things will never be as they once were. Events do change the pattern of one's life, don't they?'

'Yes, they may very well do that, Alicia. But the thing is that I am certainly not going to recreate history.'

'I don't understand what you mean, Hassan,' she told him, and, gazing down at the entwined fingers, she tightened her own.

'I expect you do understand. You might have been told that I am half English, and that in my travels I go sometimes to England. Both of which are true. But my mother hated Cairo—so I have had the experience of the results of mixed cultures. I have also no intention of repeating my father's mistake, because the desert is my heritage and Egypt is my country. And will remain that way.'

'Why wouldn't they remain so, Hassan?' Alicia smiled up at him, adding, 'For heaven's sake, just look at you, attractive beyond anyone's imagining. You would only have to raise one beckoning finger to have half the women whose features grace the world's picture pages, and . . . be able to keep them too.'

'But I have had any number of those women—and that in the Biblical sense too—and not one of them raised my heartbeat one decibel. Whereas... But I am not going into that! Look, I've told you about an invitation I have for you. Would you like to share tomorrow with me and go out on the water in a felucca? We could sail upriver and maybe stop for you to see some ruins, have lunch on the boat, and be home by four o'clock.'

As only silence answered him he said a little curtly, 'Never mind, it's almost midnight, and once that strikes who knows what the following minutes may bring? I'll take you home now.'

Breath caught in her throat, Alicia made herself speak. Never thinking that such an invitation would be extended, she said now carefully, 'Thank you, my lord Hassan, I'd be delighted to accept.'

The man laughed, and said, 'When you do do something, you do it handsomely, Alicia.' He picked up the entwined hands and, turning them, kissed the white blue-veined wrist the other side of her apricot arm.

Alicia found that that so unexpected, so small caress caused her very bones to melt. She swayed towards him and, reaching out to hold her, an arm clasped tightly. She went into him, her head thrown back, fair hair cascading over the silk-clad arm. She felt the shudder, the ripple which went through the body holding hers. She heard him say, the voice strange, husky, 'You understand, Alicia,' and, opening her eyes, she looked into blazing emerald brilliance. She heard him say again, 'You do understand that if we continue on. . . . we will come to the point of no return.'

Unspeaking, her sense of normal living gone with the wind, she only nodded, and found her feet swung up on to the couch, her body deposited among the cushions,

his own long body coming to lie beside her. His lips came
down to rest upon her own, gently, not with any heavy
demand, just moving easily back and forth as if
searching. She moved, stretching to clasp hands behind
his neck, and encircling them with only silence as gentle
lovemaking turned to want, need, with passion leaping
between them like a blazing, burning forest fire.

A hand travelling down the exposed throat met and
pushed aside the soft neckline of her blouse, then moved
with only the lightest of fingertips over the white mounds
now left bare.

Fragile, hardly touching, they still brought to every
nerve-end the jolt of hard desire. Without volition she
arched her body into the one looming above her and,
as if this small accepting movement had released a different, heavier emotion, that hand moved across her
breasts, down slowly through the hollow of her hips,
and out over thighs covered with unyielding linen. It
stopped, halted as cool bare skin came to meet it.

She knew the words he was murmuring against her
lips were entering her memory, but she didn't want to
know, and wasn't even thinking. She was only aware of
the man whose body was now enfolding hers; of heart-
beats thudding against her breast that were like the
thunder of hooves she had heard only this afternoon.

Then abruptly, as both hands and lips began to weave
their own kind of magic, she was caught up and carried
into a dimension she had not known existed. She went
gladly to meet the scorching, branding caresses of a desire
that was all-consuming. She didn't know she called out,
'Hassan,' in a tone she also wouldn't recognise.

She wasn't aware, either, of a buzzing that went on
and on; but then she was, as the man whose arms were
enfolding her went still... frozen.

It was the telephone, of course. Hassan remained immobile, as if willing it to stop. But it continued on,

bringing to the big silent room its jarring vibrations. She jumped when the man so close to her spoke in sharp, violent Arabic. Then the body had lifted away from hers. Again she heard a curt explosion of Arabic, then seemingly questions before the receiver went down with a loud thud.

Alicia turned and buried her face in the silken cushions as he stalked back to the couch. 'Alicia...' he began, but she only burrowed deeper. His arms came across and brought her upright. 'I'm sorry,' he said, 'but we have to leave.'

'Yes, of course,' she told him, turning her face away.

He still held her tightly, but his voice carried strain as well as an unfamiliar huskiness, when he said curtly, 'Wouldn't you know it? I could kill Yusef! No one else would ring here; this is an unlisted number—but with Yusef... I have to go, and quickly.'

He must have noticed the look on her face, because a long brown finger stroked gently down her cheek, and when he spoke it was in Arabic.

'What did those words mean, Hassan?'

'Oh, said in English they wouldn't mean the same. However, heart of my desire...'

Interrupting, now she did look directly at him, asking carefully, 'You did say what I thought I heard...'

Hassan laughed softly and the brown finger passed gently over her lips. 'Yes, I probably did,' he answered, then went on, 'I also think perhaps I might have to start rethinking the whole situation. But not in this place which still carries the airwaves of a lovemaking I didn't intend; a lovemaking which showed me a different kind of loving altogether.

'Now go and make yourself presentable to walk through an hotel foyer, but be quick. I have to go.'

So she returned to the gleaming bathroom and, gazing at the face reflected back at her from the mirror, she murmured, 'I look even worse than I did last night.' So, dragging a comb hurriedly through her hair, she ran a small puff over flushed and shining cheeks, then lipsticked her lips in fuchsia, hiding the burning poppy-scarlet which told its own story. She could do nothing about her eyes, shadow-hazed still with the passion, the desire that had played about her entire being.

Back again in the large room, she saw Hassan turning from the phone. He looked her over, said, 'Good,' and gave her a smile of such tenderness that her very bones seemed to melt. All he said, however, was, 'I've got to hurry. Come along!'

She went along. The keeper of the gate had arrived; the long black limousine was pulling up as they stepped outside. Ali was out immediately to open the door, then just as swiftly he was back inside to sit beside two other unfamiliar men.

The glass partition between them was raised, she saw even without properly noticing things, the world, the at-mosphere around her not yet completely registering. Everything had happened so quickly: that passionate lovemaking, that unexpected phone call summoning Hassan.

He said, and his smile this time was rueful, 'Time seems to be against us, doesn't it, Alicia? Last night! And now! Still, concerning now, I don't know if this summons was a good thing or a bad one. It certainly led to one result, however. Because if it had not come...' Alicia waited for him to continue, but Hassan had lapsed into silence.

She asked, a little hesitantly, 'Has something happened? Has there been some trouble, Hassan?'

An abrupt laugh came from the man beside her. 'Don't sound so tragic, Alicia. There is of course nothing wrong. We are the ben Amarna and there is always a guard on Yusef, but Allah help me, I'd like to throttle him. Look,

I have to go. I'll call for you at ten tomorrow. Good night!'

Alicia found herself outside on the footpath without really knowing how she had got there, the big car swiftly departing out of sight. She turned to enter the hotel, thinking that this wasn't like Hassan at all—and found Ali beside her. Of course! She said, as she had done at the Hilton in Cairo, 'There is no need . . .'

'My lord said to see you upstairs.'

Knowing it was no use arguing, Alicia went upstairs with her guard in attendance. She said thank you, and, unlocking the door, closed it behind her.

She found her aunt sitting upright in a chair by the window, the inevitable cup of tea in her hand. 'You should be in bed, Aunt Em,' Alicia told her, gazing fondly at her. 'It is well after midnight, you know.'

'For that matter, after midnight is late for a young girl returning from a date—and that with someone she had only just met.' The shrewd old eyes looked the young girl up and down, then asked softly, 'Did you enjoy Karnak, love?'

'Karnak . . .' Alicia's hand flew to her mouth. Surely she couldn't have forgotten the magic that was Karnak. Especially experiencing it with whom she had. 'Oh, yes, Karnak . . .' she told her aunt. 'It was absolutely fantastic. Was your bridge as wonderful?'

'Well, I enjoyed it. Just four of us. But I tell you, it's a mystery how we got together. I don't know, and neither did they!'

Oh, blame it on the ben Amarna, went the reflection through Alicia's mind, but all she said was, 'Did you win? You usually do.'

A hand went up and down in a waving movement. 'Shall we say,' her aunt told her with some amusement, 'that I didn't lose? I really did enjoy tonight. They were very good players.'

Alicia went over and placed an arm around the thin shoulders. She bent down and kissed the wrinkled cheek, saying, 'I'm so pleased for you.' Then, straightening up, she said, 'I'm for bed. I think jet lag is more than catching up with me.' She collected her nightdress on the way to the bathroom, and heard her aunt ask, 'Did you have any dinner?'

Flipping a hand behind her, Alicia said, 'Yes, thank you, I did. I was given a meal, but what it consisted of I couldn't tell you.' She sidled into the bathroom.

She didn't look at the face her mirror would show. She didn't want to remember how it had been the last time she had seen it reflected back at her. She washed and even creamed her face, dawdling about until there was nothing else she could find to do.

The bedroom was in darkness, she saw thankfully when she returned, so, moving to the big window, she flung back the curtains and slid it open a little. Outside was still busy, she saw, gazing down beneath her. Cars swishing past, horse-drawn buggies clip-clopping along. Egyptians in their long gowns sauntering about laughing and talking among themselves as if it were five o'clock in the afternoon, not progressing towards another new day. There was no moonlight on the Nile, but the glitter of starshine was there. Alicia turned and climbed into bed.

Curled into a ball, sheet pulled up to her cheek, she decided not to think about the love-scene or the man who had participated in it. He was leaving Luxor tomorrow, and in two days' time, if he was right about their horses selling, she would also be leaving. At Cairo they would make arrangements about Johnny, then go home.

Caught within an attraction acknowledged by both, it had been Hassan who had behaved impeccably—she certainly had not. Well, she would not behave so again.

She would go out on this famous river tomorrow and enjoy the day which Hassan had scrounged, and for whatever reason had given to her.

Whether he was married—and, him being who he was, who would know?—or if he was committed to another woman, no longer mattered. It was finished, this unexpected meeting with a man like him. She acknowledged, however, that these few days spent in Egypt would remain a memory not easily forgotten; but she was wise enough to accept that their culture, their worlds were far apart. Hadn't he intimated as much to her, especially when dogmatically forbidding her to go to the horse-fair in the desert.

She turned restlessly, burrowing her head deeper into the pillow. Then something she had temporarily forgotten, but which her consciousness had not, showed her Karnak. And Karnak with all its overwhelming magic was suddenly encircling her. She smiled happily on seeing again an effulgent living oasis rising from the bare desert sands, and remembered gratefully that enchanting voice which had sounded all around her. She drifted deeply into oblivion.

A different sort of voice calling awakened her, but tiredly she went to put an arm across her eyes. It came again, strong, an unknown sound. Eyes opened wide now, she saw a new day through the open window, and heard the voice echoing for a last time. Of course, she thought, remembering where she was. From some high minaret a muezzin was calling the faithful to prayer. Sending a glance to her sleeping aunt, Alicia slipped out of bed.

Standing within the open window in only a short nightdress, she gazed down and across. There were no cars or horse-drawn carriages travelling along the street beneath her now. However, the waterway was busy, with feluccas sailing upriver, and down. Also there was one big launch parting the water below it as it sped swiftly across to the left bank. She had decided last night that this land was different from her land. Well, it wasn't, she thought now, acknowledging the deep azure sky, the golden sunshine that was a replica of her own. Only the people and culture were different. She closed the window and turned into the room.

Seeing her aunt was now awake, she went and sat beside her on the bed. She said, taking hold of the thin hand, 'I know you won't mind, you never do, but I still feel guilty...'

'Guilty, Alicia? I don't like the sound of that. Just tell me and put me out of my alarm.'

Alicia laughed, she said, 'I am spending the day on the river, darling Aunt Em. So can I arrange a guided tour for you?'

'No, you can't! You know I can always amuse myself, but tell me, are you going out with that man; that Sheikh Something or other.'

'Yes...'

'You know what you are doing, I suppose.'

'Yes...' Alicia still spoke only the one word. Then she did continue on. 'It is only for today. He is leaving Luxor at five o'clock.'

'Do you like him, Alicia?'

'Oh, Aunt Em,' suddenly Alicia was laughing. 'Of course I do. He is the most vividly handsome man I have ever seen—or am likely to ever see. And he could just give a beckoning smile to have any woman interested. Although——' Suddenly she was thinking of him as she spoke, of the charisma that patterned the air-waves around him, of the way he acted. 'Although,' she repeated, 'he doesn't expect any of his decisions...his commands to be disregarded.

'It is as well,' she went on, 'that I won't ever see him again after today. Because I might...could very well be

one of those women I mentioned, and that wouldn't do
at all. For, apart from our different heritages, I even
expect I might be a little frightened of him.'

'Frightened of him?' Her aunt's tone was in-
credulous. 'You can't really mean that, Alicia . . . in this
day and age you can't use the word "frightened".'

'Yes, well,' replied her niece with a rueful smile, 'just
take it that I am pleased somewhere inside me that I
won't have to put it to the test.'

Her aunt shook her head, then said forcefully, 'I need
a cup of tea after hearing that.'

'I'll get it for you, and then have first go at the
bathroom,' her niece told her placatingly.

So they bathed and dressed and went for breakfast on
this last day but one in Luxor. Alicia was cleaning her
teeth when a knock came upon the door. She looked in
alarm at her froth-coated mouth and hurriedly washed
it away. Still, it couldn't be Hassan, it was only just after
nine, so, taking up a small towel, she went into the
bedroom. She said to the figure standing by the window,
'You could have answered it, Aunt Em.'

'No, I couldn't. The telephone could have been used
for ordinary things. Knocks coming on our door presage
something out of the ordinary. I am certainly too old to
be getting involved in such goings-on.'

Alicia patted her lips dry, and moved to the door. For
the second time on answering this kind of summons, she
stood motionless. An unknown Arab stood there, one
certainly not dressed in the colours she was familiar with.
He handed her an envelope. Thanking him, she glanced
at it and saw that it was addressed to Miss Seacombe.

Not for her, thought Alicia, and was beginning to
move inside when the man said, as Ali had done, 'My
lady would like an answer, please.'

So she reentered the room and said a little ma-
liciously, 'For you, my dear Aunt Em.'

As if expecting a snake might jump out of it, that lady opened the envelope cautiously, then said, 'It is an invitation to lunch—from someone signed Soraya ben Amarna.'

'That damned Hassan and his manners!' exclaimed Alicia, then added, 'You are going to accept I suppose.'

'Yes of course. Go and tell him so, love.'

So walking to the open door, Alicia said thank you, and that yes, her aunt would be delighted.

'Well, I don't expect any more knocks—except for Hassan's,' said Alicia, returning to check herself in the mirror. The tight cream linen trousers ending an inch above her ankles were OK, she had decided, but not the top that went with them. That was too revealing for today's trip. Not knowing who would be on the felucca, she had played it safe by donning a big, loose-knit sloppy joe of the same deep cream which came to below her hips. Finishing her outfit with heavy white sneakers and socks, she looked modern, with that uncared-for look.

'I don't believe it,' she exclaimed, as a further knock sounded. 'It's not Hassan. Knowing him, he would be exactly on time, and this is too early, so it's your turn to answer,' she told her aunt, and went on outlining her lips with colour.

Her aunt just laughed at her.

She wasn't just astounded, she was almost paralysed when she opened the door. 'I am the Sheikh Yusef of the ben Amarna,' said the man standing there.

'Yes, I know,' Alicia managed to say, when she could reply to this fierce, autocratic, almost frightening young man.

'How could you? You have not met me,' an accented voice said in English.

'I might not have actually met you; but I have seen you. In the airport at Athens.'

'Oh, it surely wasn't you I looked at, was it?' he asked, and laughed.

'No, it was not! Or I wouldn't be standing here talking to you now.'

Good heavens. Her hand flew to her mouth. What was there about these ben Amarna men that made her act so uncharacteristically? Normally she was a polite well-brought-up young girl. So now she said, thinking of her manners, 'How do you do, Sheikh Yusef? I am happy to meet you.' She couldn't make herself continue. She couldn't say, why are you here? What do you want?

'Thank you,' he told her, without saying he was happy to meet her. He then added, 'I have been ordered to come and apologise!'

'Apologise...' She made her mouth, which had fallen open, close itself. She began again, 'Why should you apologise, Sheikh Yusef? And who could order you?'

'Oh, my cousin can when he is in the sort of temper he was in last night. He said I had interrupted your dinner, your evening.'

She couldn't stop it, the burning tide of scarlet that washed from throat to cheeks. Good heavens. Interrupted her dinner!

The eyes of the fierce young man looking at her saw it—and understood it, she was sure. For they were abruptly hooded, and for a brief fleeting moment it could have been Hassan standing there. She shook her head.

'So, as I spoilt your evening, I am to come and abjectly apologise.'

Suddenly, other memories gone with the wind, Alicia was laughing. She told him, 'I accept your apology, but really, Sheikh Yusef, not to knock your English, I simply don't believe you have the least idea what the word "abjectly" means. Especially when applied to you.'

He smiled at her, this man she would have thought twice about crossing, and informed her, 'I don't! Still, if it pleases my cousin, that's all that matters. But now I have to please my father, and there is a helicopter waiting.' He didn't say goodbye, or give any other kind of leave-taking. He just inclined his head and, turning, was gone, his two bodyguards in their attentive places.

CHAPTER SIX

WHEN for the third time that morning a knock sounded upon their door, Alicia took a deep breath and picked up her shoulder-bag. This couldn't be anyone else but Hassan, she thought, and said, 'Come along, Aunt Em, and meet him.'

Also for the third time that morning, she stood silent, unable to make herself speak.

It wasn't so with her visitor. 'Good morning, Alicia,' he said, 'Shouldn't it be you, though, on receiving a guest, to be the one giving the greeting?'

'Yes... but you are not what I expected.'

'For Allah's sake, not again! Tell me who or what you did expect.'

'Sorry... Of course I was expecting you—this time—but not looking the way you do.'

'First things first. Why "this time?" Who has come here that you didn't expect?' The brilliant emerald eyes had gone from a smiling expectation to hard questioning.

'Yes, well,' Alicia found herself getting angry too, and said sharply, 'We have had two callers this morning, and I expected neither of them.'

'You can tell me who they were later, but we'll discuss that second thing you mentioned now. What did you mean about me "looking the way I do"? When...escorts called for you in Australia to go sailing, surely they were dressed as I am, and looking the way I do?'

She didn't know what to answer so said carefully, 'No one has ever come calling for me looking the way you do.'

75

'Then that's just too bad. This is classed as the recognised dress for social sailing in Egypt—or, for that matter, anywhere else in the world I have gone on the water.' Hauteur coloured the crisp English voice.

'For heaven's sake, Hassan. I wasn't speaking about dress. Of course you would be correct. Being you, you would always be so.' She gazed at the immaculate white linen trousers, the striped blue and white knit shirt, the white canvas sneakers and socks. He certainly looked dressed for sailing—as if he was there to be photographed for a glossy advertisement.

'Certainly no man looking the way you do has ever come calling for me, and I don't mean that in the dress sense. I meant it entirely otherwise.'

Pausing, not knowing what else to say, she then noticed incredulously the tinge of red that came to colour the bronzed cheeks. Her hand flew upwards to prevent other words emerging.

'Very well, Alicia,' said a cool, crisp voice, 'leaving me and my attire out of the discussion, why have you been so busy with callers this morning?'

'Firstly, it was your... an invitation for Aunt Em.'

'Oh, yes, that would be from my stepmother. However, I thought she would just phone.'

'Well, she didn't phone,' replied Alicia a little tartly— she was tired of all this. 'Then,' she was continuing on, and unexpectedly collapsed into giggles. 'There was Yusef.'

'Yusef? This morning? I expected...' A frown came to settle between those emerald eyes.

'Well, he was here, Hassan, and did you really *order* him to come and apologise—abjectly?'

'I don't remember what I told him to do. I was so blazing angry...'

'But *abjectly*...for someone like him to use such a word. I think he is a frightening young man.'

'Frightening or not, to me last night he was merely a damned young nuisance, and as I have said I could willingly have throttled him. However... However,' repeated that so assured, so handsome man before her, 'I have to—and he knows it—accord him the respect I owe to the heir of the paramount chief of the ben Amarna. Did he apologise?'

'Oh, yes. Because, he said, he had interrupted my dinner.'

'What would you have expected me to tell him he interrupted?' enquired Hassan, and she saw wicked amusement grow in those magnetic eyes.

Ignoring his words, aware of the tide of scarlet that had flown to stain both throat and cheeks as she remembered what *had* been interrupted, she asked a little breathlessly, 'But abjectly! I did ask him if he knew what it meant. He blithely told me he didn't. That, as you had ordered it, that was what he was doing. Also, that he was now going to obey another order from a different source—his father's.'

'Has he gone, I wonder? I wanted...'

'I expect he has. He said there was a helicopter waiting. Do you, a desert tribe, use helicopters all the time? I would have thought it was horses...or camels.'

A smile came to light up that handsome face, gaiety showing alongside of amusement. 'Oh, yes,' he exclaimed, 'we do have horses and camels—and use them too. Now, shall we go?'

'Yes, but first, I'd like you to meet my aunt.'

His glance went over her shoulder, and she swung round. Aunt Em was standing there. 'My Aunt Emily, Sheikh Hassan,' she introduced them.

He half started to raise a hand, and Alicia thought it was to use the formal Arabic gesture of respect towards a superior—or the elderly. However, almost at once he said only, 'How do you do, Miss Seacombe? I am happy to meet you.'

'I am happy finally to meet you also, Sheikh Hassan.'

'To see if I have—or haven't—two horns and a tail, I expect,' came the words from the tall figure so close to her.

Alicia gasped.

'Yes, that too,' replied her incorrigible aunt. 'Also, I wanted to see if a certain description could possibly be true.'

'And was it?' She was asked, and there was more than laughter in those magnetic eyes now, Alicia saw. They were dancing with wicked amusement.

'I suspect it might have been. Wouldn't that be right, Alicia?'

'I would say that we have been indulging in too much personal conversation,' said her niece sharply, while thinking that at her age it was about time she had learnt not to blush. Never mind Hassan talking about killing Yusef. *She* could willingly kill her aunt at the present moment.

'OK.' Hassan half raised a hand in farewell, saying, 'We'll be off. I hope you enjoy your lunch, Miss Seacombe——'

'And that reminds me——' began the elderly lady, as she went to interrupt.

'And that reminds me also that time and tide wait for no man.' Alicia's elbow was lightly taken and she was being turned into the hallway. Apparently, Hassan had no intention of discussing lunches.

Walking beside him down the long corridor, the circumspect yard or so between them, Alicia noticed that this time there was no one waiting at the lifts. They descended in silence, her companion leaning negligently against a wall. As she had done once before in this very lift, she gazed surreptitiously across at him, and suddenly, without expecting it, completely out of the blue, she felt the jolt of a heartbeat missing.

Glancing swiftly away from that handsome bronzed countenance, she told herself and her missing heartbeat astringently, 'I *know* he is outstandingly attractive. I *know* he can be nice as well as...' She tore her memory away from two other occasions, and muttered again to herself, 'But he can also be arrogant and frightening. So I am only going to go out and treat this as if it is an ordinary date... and enjoy myself.'

She didn't even smile wryly while registering the words she had said. Ordinary date! She actually started, however, when he spoke, coolly in crisp English, but with that wicked pirate's smile seen once before this morning, 'Well, shall we go out and walk through this hotel as if we owned it?'

'With all the experience I have had of you,' she replied tartly, 'I expect you probably do.' And heard him laughing as he stepped from the lift beside her. So they began their walk through the foyer, and of course towards a familiar figure waiting by the entrance. Ali fell in behind his master.

Halted on the footpath by three riders trotting past, tourists by the looks of them, Alicia glanced first at the horses, not the riders. Bringing her gaze back while wondering about her own animals, wondering if... She encountered a satirical smile. 'I don't want to hear the word "horses" spoken today. Now, shall we go?'

Yes, asked in that tone, she would certainly go—even if a trifle mutinously. After all, tomorrow her horses were to be sold, and of course she was worried and hoping they would sell well. 'I *really* don't like you, Hassan,' she muttered.

Whether he heard her words or not, the man now walking carelessly across the road beside her said, 'I have told you, Alicia, that I always only speak the truth. That

I always only say what I mean; and I have told you that your animals will do well. Now...'

Ali opened the door of the now familiar limousine, and once settled inside Hassan told her, 'We haven't far to go. Just to our own landing further along.'

'Just to your *own* landing?' replied Alicia deciding to be difficult.

'Yes, of course. Don't firms in your country own landings upon rivers—and even upon oceans...?'

'Oh...' Alicia flung up her hands '...upon oceans too. I might have expected it.' Hearing the words echoing around the small, enclosing space, Alicia was suddenly wildly angry with herself. Why was she behaving this way?

Her companion only laughed, saying, 'I really don't know about oceans. That is not my department. Still, most likely we have.'

'Oh, you...you...' Unable to find words strong enough to express her tumbling thoughts, Alicia lapsed into silence. At least there were unknown and strange sights to gaze at outside her window.

The way, as Hassan had intimated, was not long. Ali opened their door. However, he didn't take up his usual post, but skipped before them along a hard-planked jetty extending out over the river. He was untying ropes as Hassan held out a hand to help her aboard the vessel. Not on to a deck of any ordinary old ship, went the thought laughingly through her mind, but on to one with the romantic name of a felucca.

Her hand still held tightly, Hassan was smiling down his wicked, piratical smile at her, saying, 'Come into my parlour. It can be used for the same purpose as my quarters once were. Wasn't it you who told me that, Alicia? So I thought I would reciprocate in telling you this could be just another venue.'

Understanding what he was saying, knowing his intentions were so different, she gave to him a radiant, happy smile. And was disconcerted when lids fell over those eyes which had just before only glinted amusement at her. All that could be discerned now was a gleaming emerald slit beneath dark brows drawn together.

Then abruptly they were wide open again, and she drew a deep, relieved breath. Everything was all right. She had just imagined it wasn't.

Still holding her hand, Hassan drew her across the scrubbed-plank deck towards some canvas chairs under an awning. Dropping into one, Alicia pulled off her hat. 'That's heavenly!' she exclaimed blissfully, on feeling the wind of their passing waft through their enclosed space.

The man looming above her, an arm clamped about an upright, looked down at the fair, shining hair set tumbling; at the girl waving happily at another felucca skimming before the wind as it charged past. His hand clenched tightly on a rail behind.

'It's not fair,' exclaimed Alicia gazing up at him. 'Why is it going faster than us?'

Dropping down beside her and stretching long, white-clad legs upon the planks beneath them, Hassan also straightened dark black brows which had been drawn together. Now, back to his smiling holiday self, he told her, 'It's a working felucca, Alicia, carrying cargo downriver. *We* are sailing for pleasure and going upriver where there are some ruins scattered about. I thought you might like to indulge that romantic side of yourself by exploring them.'

'Oh, yes, I would. Thank you, Hassan. I'll always remember Karnak, you know.'

'Only Karnak! Not an escort who took you there?' Then, before she could reply, he said, 'No, sorry. . .' and the wicked gleam that had surfaced in those magnetic

eyes while he had spoken those words vanished as he
continued, 'That wasn't supposed to be on the agenda.'

What could she say? Of course she would remember
who escorted her to Karnak.

'And, speaking of agendas, I'll get Mustapha to fetch
us a cold drink. You'd like one, wouldn't you?' asked
her companion.

'Mustapha! Is he here? I thought this was to be a picnic
day.'

'So it is to be a picnic day. And for that we need food.
Hence Mustapha.'

'Truly, Hassan?' Alicia was laughing directly across
at him. 'Haven't you ever had a picnic where you have
had to do things for yourself?'

'No, I haven't! And I don't propose to begin—especially not today.'

'Truly, Hassan?' Repeating the two words, Alicia
shook her head, unable to understand those sentiments.
She told him, 'Well, in my humble way, I have loved
packing for picnics and always enjoyed them—even
sharing our lunch with ants too—sometimes.'

'Enjoy this just for me, then—without the ants,' said
a voice carrying an altogether different timbre, and,
turning to the indolently lounging figure in the chair
beside her, she saw that Mustapha was there, carrying
a tray of glasses. He smiled as he handed her one, and
she felt the coldness of it, and the clink of ice.

Raising it to her mouth, Alicia took a sip, and then
another one. 'It's delicious,' she said, turning to the long
supine figure in the angled canvas chair.

Alicia thought that the half-shut eyes were not hooded
to hide an expression as they sometimes were. His whole
lazing figure suggested tiredness. She wondered how late
he had been involved in Yusef's affairs.

She made herself ask, if only absently, 'You said you wouldn't be leaving Egypt this afternoon, Hassan. Are you going to the ben Amarna headquarters?'

'No.' Turning slightly, he smiled lazily, caressingly at her just as if he too were only speaking absently. 'I'm going out to the far desert. I work with water, Alicia. Trying to improve sparse supplies in our far-flung oases.'

'Oh...' She gazed again at the figure stretched out beside her, then continued, 'I've always wondered why there is water in some places and not in...'

He turned to her, that wicked, piratical gleam in his eyes. 'It is a mystery the boffins are all interested in trying to solve,' he murmured, and then leant back again.

She looked at him, at the hand lying there so casually between them. It was just a hand, but unexpectedly, completely out of the blue, she felt a surge of emotion welling. She had told herself, and believed it, that there was an attraction—even a strong attraction between them. But a love-affair was something else. To be in love, you... She gazed at the hand, at the long, strong, bronzed outline of it, and her glass slipped from suddenly nerveless fingers.

Gazing at it lying shattered on the deck, she then looked blindly at the man who turned so suddenly to her at the sound of its falling. What he saw in her face made him exclaim, 'Come along, Alicia, we'll stand in the prow and watch for some ruins in which to go exploring.' His voice might have sounded even, casual, if you didn't take note of the strain deep within it. He didn't put out a hand to help her up; he stood gazing out over the water.

'Leave it,' he told her harshly, as she went to pick up broken glass.

So, walking beside the measured footsteps, she went to stand in the prow of the felucca. Here the wind was much stronger and her hair was soon a tangled mess.

Glancing out over this so famous river, which was almost as busy as a motorway, Alicia allowed it to slide past her without awareness. This man beside her, experienced, knowledgeable, had told her so definitely that this day was to be a holiday-time. Still, she thought angrily, he needn't have organised it, so he must have wanted to.

Suddenly, though, she pushed all her angry thoughts away—with also that other one which had jumped so unexpectedly out at her. She knew... she had known he was leaving. What had just surfaced within her made no difference. She turned to speak to him, and found him watching her with a frown, no, with almost a scowl that sent those magnetic eyes half shut.

She said, without thinking, without volition, sending her radiant smile up at him, 'It doesn't matter...' and heard him reply.

'Yes, it does. I should have more sense...' Then he stopped speaking as a presence materialised beside them.

'It is hot, Miss Seacombe, here in Egypt, and you need liquid—and a hat,' said Mustapha, handing her a glass without mentioning the other one lying shattered upon the deck. He also presented her with her hat.

She accepted both, and smiled at him, saying, 'This drink is delicious, Mustapha. The lord Hassan says he doesn't know what it consists of. I find its taste is strange to me, however.'

'We don't have a lot of citrus fruit growing here, Miss Seacombe, so we improvise with the fruits and plant derivatives we do have.'

'Well, whatever you have found to use in this mixture is very successful. Thank you, Mustapha.'

'I am pleased that you like it,' he replied, and turned from her to offer the tray to Hassan, who went to wave it away. Then, as Mustapha spoke softly in Arabic, he took up a glass instead. Silent footsteps departed.

Alicia crammed the hat upon her head, thinking that her hair would be sticking out like broom straws. Oh, well...

'Someone is waving to you,' murmured Hassan.

Glancing up quickly from watching the water part beneath their passage, Alicia saw a launch with passengers waving wildly at them. No one was familiar, but she waved gaily back as tourists do. She decided a little wryly that appearances could be so deceptive. All those people saw were two attractive people silhouetted against blue skies under blazing sunlight, skimming along a famous river under pristine white sails. Little did they know!

She turned slightly, gazing up at her companion. She found him looking down at her, and outlining those sculptured lips was a lopsided smile. He asked, 'Well, what now?'

So it was her asking carefully back, raising her glass first to swallow, 'You said once that you went away. Why did you, when you also told me you loved all this.' Her hand flew out in a throwaway gesture, not only to the river, but to the land surrounding it. She paused, wariness of him taking over, then, flashing a quick, startled look at him, she saw again that wicked, dancing gleam lighting up his eyes.

Damn him, she thought. I *will* ask him, then. She said, 'Where did you go?'

'I went to Cambridge!'

Brow furrowed for a moment, she was silent, then asked, 'Cambridge, England?'

'Is there another Cambridge?' he asked, astonishment in his voice, an eyebrow raised sky-high, and she knew he was laughing at her.

'Yes, there certainly is. And you know it.' Well, he had given her permission to ask, so she did, 'What did you do at Cambridge?'

'I took an engineering degree.'

'Truly?' she began. This was so far from her imagining. She then saw laughter again colour that bronzed, handsome countenance as she used one of her favourite words.

'Yes, truly,' was all he replied, however.

She looked him over from top to toe, this man whose clothes shouted elegance, perfection, thinking that they also shouted leisured wealth. His attitude too, since she had known him, had also shown only authority, brusqueness, and the wanting of his own way—and getting it.

She told him astringently, 'You don't look like any engineer.'

'There we go again,' he replied sharply, then added, 'Have you ever seen an engineer? Tell me what they look like?'

'No, I can't remember that I ever have. But I'm sure they wouldn't look like you now. And...' she paused before saying categorically '...I can't imagine you sitting at a desk poring over papers, either...'

'There, you see, Alicia,' he broke in curtly. 'That shows you don't know me. I can sit at a desk and pore over papers with the best of men—to get what I want! And I wanted that degree... Oh, not to get the degree as such...' his hand flew out in a negative gesture '...because I will never have to go out into the workplace...'

Gazing at him, she saw only his eyes staring blankly into the far distance, his entire being having no part in this surrounding scene; and knew that she had lost him. She felt a chill even in this bright, hot sunshine. Then he was back, smiling down at her, saying, 'Water is my passion and I wanted to know all about it—what it does, from where it originates; how one can find its source to harness it... Oh, good heavens, I'm being boring. Sorry...'

'No, you're not being boring. You're talking about something you believe in, and also...' She smiled up at him. 'Dare I tell you that, besides your being an engineer, I remember what a wonderful horseman you are too.'

'Oh, Alicia.' Hassan was laughing now. 'There is nothing in being able to tell a horse what to do. We sit on them from babyhood upwards... Apropos that, are you a wonderful horsewoman?'

'Of course!'

Angrily she saw that he was not only laughing at her now, but nearly doubled up with mirth. 'There is no false modesty about that answer, anyway,' he told her when he could speak naturally.

'Of course there isn't. I have ridden in, and won, too many equestrian events.'

His hand went up in the universal gesture of pax, and he asked her, 'When you sell——' not *if* you sell, she noticed '—this Dark Shadow, are you going to get a new mount?'

'No. I'm leaving home and going to Brisbane. There is nothing I can do there now. There will only be a few horses for Grandfather to play around with. So...I'm off to the city to find a career.' She didn't add that it was a decision only arrived at half an hour or so ago.

'To the city! By yourself?' Again a scowl came to rest between those glinting emerald eyes.

'Of course by myself.' Puzzled, Alicia turned to face him. 'I'm almost twenty-one. Quite old by today's standards. Also, I know Brisbane, and have contacts there.' She smiled at him as she spoke, and then, her tone changing, exclaimed, 'Oh, look, it's you they're waving to now.'

Gaily dressed, happy and exuberant, a crowd of tourists were gathered together in the stern of a passing felucca. They were wildly waving and calling out greetings across the water. Absently, Hassan waved back, then turned quickly away as Ali called out.

He nodded and gestured assent, so Ali sent the felucca in towards the bank. Sailing closer to what they were both looking at, Alicia saw that there were indeed ruins, or buildings of some sort further in from the river.

Hassan asked, turning away from their landmark, 'Would you like to come along and wash your hands, Alicia? Or...' here he grinned down at her '...even comb your hair.'

Following him down a short flight of steps, she found she was entering some sort of living-room with a table bolted to one side, and a broad bench along the other. Exactly in the middle was a door. Hassan gestured to it, saying, 'Come along up when you're ready.'

It was only a small two-bunk room with a tiny bathroom opening from it. So she washed her hands, rummaged in her shoulder-bag for sunscreen and used it sparingly upon her face. The lipstick she also used sparingly. Lastly, she combed the tangles from her hair, and, with it smooth and shining, placed her hat carefully over it.

Then, taking the deep breath she always needed when she was going to meet Hassan, she took her camera, then left the bag lying on the bunk.

Hassan was throwing tying ropes to Ali when she arrived back, but then turned as his bodyguard hauled the felucca close. He looked at her and said absently, 'It's a shame to cover that hair.' He then added sharply as her mouth almost dropped open, 'Now don't pretend you don't know it's lovely, and...' The timbre as well as the language changed, the words coming to her in harsh Arabic as he finished the broken sentence.

'You are not fair, Hassan. I can't say things in another language that you can't understand, when I would sometimes very much like to!'

'Would you like to be able to do so? But it is really not necessary, Alicia. I always know what you are thinking—what you would very much like to say!'

'You might think you do, but you don't,' she told him angrily.

He laughed softly down at her and reached out long fingers to take her hand. 'Yes, I do,' he told her definitely, and turned the hand he held. As he had done last night he kissed the white, blue-veined wrist the other side of an apricot arm.

Unlike last night, however, his lips didn't remain static. They moved up and inch or so, then down an inch or so. Eyes closed, bones melting as that so light touch sent ripples of emotion, desire surging, she collapsed towards him. The hand which had been enfolding hers so lightly now clamped tight, holding her firmly upright. Blue eyes, hazed and shadowed, opened to look directly into the fire of emerald green.

He swore—of course she knew it was swearing—as again harsh Arabic sounded about their two immobile figures. Then he had turned and jumped down, to stand speaking to Ali and another Egyptian in a long gown.

CHAPTER SEVEN

ALICIA put out a hand to grasp the railing protecting the boat's side, then, as he turned, holding out a hand to help her, she gazed stonily at him, and cursed Hassan, and then Johnny for getting hurt, and bringing her into Hassan's orbit. What dark star circling about or above her own had caused him to be in that one particular place, at that one particular time...? She thought, as it had been thought since time began, 'It's not fair.'

Gravely he returned her look, then said carefully, 'Come and explore, Alicia.'

So she put her hand into the one this Arab princeling held out to her, and decided with no reservations whatsoever that she was glad she wouldn't see him again after today. She would close her mind completely to this country—and the people she had met in it.

She would—as she had been told to—enjoy today, and these ruins. She would talk and laugh, and take pictures, and be just a tourist.

So, in the bright, hot sunshine under a cerulean sky as the one at home usually was, she walked beside him towards this tumble of ruins. Trailing a hand absently over hard granite stone as she passed one waist-high boulder, she found that in spite of herself she was interested.

Further along, lightly touching what seemed writing and figures carved into the stone, she brought out her camera. 'I am allowed to photograph?' she asked the silent form at her side.

'Be my... be our guest,' was all he replied.

So she took her snaps, and as she again allowed her fingers to slide carefully back and forth over engraved granite, she asked what the signs meant.

Hassan smiled that lop-sided smile he sometimes gave, then added, 'The only hieroglyphics I can read are those concerning engineering scrawled on a blackboard.'

'I bet you could understand them too,' he was answered tartly. And, hearing herself speak these words, Alicia muttered, 'Good, I'm getting back to normal.'

A tourist wending his way down from the other party, exploring as they were, stopped to talk, and, moving slightly, Alicia focused her camera. There came a little click.

'I hope I don't look like King Kong in it. *That* wouldn't be good for any memories,' said Hassan.

Suddenly, casting away the previous minutes, allowing this lovely day, this so different and exotic place to take over her being, Alicia smiled at him, saying, 'You didn't mind?'

'No, why should I, except . . .'

'The except doesn't matter, Hassan. You have made Egypt come alive for me. As for the other, well . . . Oh, look,' Alicia changed the subject determinedly, 'there's a kind of room over on that rise. Can we go and see it?'

'Of course.' So they strolled along, the tall, handsome man and the fair young girl, acting like tourists, exchanging greetings. And, as they did so, Alicia saw Ali had closed in beside Hassan.

She grinned sardonically, then suddenly said to herself, 'Keep standing like that . . . please . . . oh, please.' For Hassan had turned to answer a question, and his face was outlined in brilliant light. She focused, and as if he knew, as if their thoughts had flown to meet across the airwaves, he remained motionless. Lowering her camera, she knew she had got the snap of a lifetime. *Her* lifetime, anyway. She was only an amateur photographer.

She said as the others moved off, 'Can I have one of you and Ali? He is almost as much a part of this time in Egypt as you are. Well, probably not almost; still...would he mind?'

Her escort glanced at his bodyguard and raised an eyebrow. The maroon and white striped burnous moved nearer, and Alicia once again focused and clicked.

With the other party leaving and having the place to themselves, Hassan placed two strong hands about her waist and swung her upwards. Alicia found she was standing on a plinth of stone and that a hand was reaching for her camera.

'You have indulged yourself all morning; now it's my turn,' said a soft, easy voice. 'No, don't look down at me. Look into the distance. I want to get all of you.'

Hassan moved back only a few paces, and she decided she might have been told to gaze into the distance, but apparently she wasn't going to be a distant figure. So, putting up a hand to shade eyes gazing into blazing sunlight, she glanced out and over the ruins towards the gleam of the river.

'Now,' ordered that still, soft voice, 'take off that hat and smile at me.'

She did pull off her hat, and, running fingers through the damp strands of hair to loosen them as she shook them free, she flung her head back to complete the process.

'There,' she informed him, 'I've done that, but I can't make myself smile to order.'

'Very well, but you can look down at me, and think that though I don't own these ruins, my ancestors might have once done, so you can smile at me as you did when we walked out of that lift, and across the foyer of the Winter Palace.'

Thinking of it, and of Hassan's actions and words before it, she did smile down at him. The smile he returned as she did as she was bade made her decide once again that he wasn't being fair. He pushed the shutter.

Then his whole expression had changed and he was laughing as he reached out arms to swing her down. He made of it no gesture of passion that could have had her clamped to his body, but a gay holiday action. Set firmly on the ground, she saw him open the camera and remove the film.

He flipped a hand at the surprised look she sent to him, saying, 'It will save you trouble. They can be dropped in this evening and delivered to you tomorrow.'

He gave a last glance around, and, watching him, Alicia saw an unfamiliar expression colouring that face, a face which more than ever now in these surroundings echoed old classical times. She also saw lids fall over those eyes of deep emerald . . . then he had swung round.

In her turn, she also gazed about her, at ruins thousands of years old, and wondered if anyone living within them all those aeons ago had felt as she did now. She grinned ironically.

'Why that kind of smile?' asked Hassan, and she started, unaware that his gaze had returned from the vast tumble of stones to settle upon her.

'Oh, just thinking,' was all she could find to reply. She wasn't going to tell *him* what she had been thinking. So she went with him to walk through this last place she would ever be with him, going down to board the felucca.

The rest of the day began with Mustapha standing beside a table set beneath an awning. It certainly wasn't set, either, for a scratch picnic meal. Silver glinted by the side of a many coloured salad reposing in its crystal receptacle, and placed before her on a plain white plate with fluted edges were cold meats which she found could almost be cut with a fork. Fruit drink was there too, in long, tall glasses, tinkling with ice. Having been seated, she muttered softly to herself, 'Come for a picnic lunch, indeed.'

So she picked up her fork, and as the felucca edged steadily into mid-channel, and then under the smallest sliver of canvas slowly sailed the Nile, she began to eat this meal set before her.

Her companion remaining silent, she gave her attention to the waterway about her; and its traffic. She couldn't help noticing, however, that her escort was merely pushing food around his plate, which seemed strange. In her experience, men were the ones who ate.

'I expect you swim and sunbathe on beaches at home, Alicia,' came words out of the silence, and Alicia thought—no, knew—that he was just trying to make conversation. So, replying, she told him carelessly, 'I swim, of course. I think most Australians do. But no, I didn't go to the beaches, as I lived out west. Ours is a vast, large country, you know.'

'Yes, I do know. At least,' here she saw thankfully that he was smiling naturally at her as he continued, 'I know from looking at a map.' He moved slightly as Mustapha came to change courses, and she saw his hand go out in a negative gesture to his still half-full plate. Mustapha took it away.

What was she to do, or say, to a man who was suddenly unapproachable? She didn't even want to pick up her spoon when Mustapha set a wide crystal bowl before her. As if sensing her mood, he told her gently, 'It's sherbet and melts in the mouth.'

So she did pick up her spoon, and found that the dessert did exactly what Mustapha had said it would do, leaving unfamiliar traces of its flavour behind. Still, even as she was eating it, she noticed that their transport was turning and thought, So we are going back. She didn't comment on it.

Then, with the appearance again of Mustapha, Hassan spoke to him. Hearing the low Arabic, Alicia sent her attention elsewhere. She was to take memories of Egypt home with her, so besides Karnak, and this man she had met here, she would take this day too.

This day with a sky arched above in deep indigo; with hot molten sunshine glinting off ripples on the water, and with that isolated stand of palms sending exquisite outflung fronds to meet the very heavens. Oh, yes, she would take a part of Egypt home with her.

She put up a hand to push back a strand of hair as a breeze from the river wafted against them, thinking how cool it was under the awning. 'It is no wonder tourists come here, Hassan,' she said softly into the silence about them. 'It's all so beautiful.'

His eyes gleamed sardonically across at her. He replied, 'Oh, yes, I accept that, but you must realise that every day is not a picnic day, and that every place is not a place to go picnicking in.'

'Well, who would think it was? Doesn't that apply to all places and countries? However, you're not going to spoil my pleasure in being given this beautiful day, this...' her hand flew out over the table with its paraphernalia spread out upon it '...so-called picnic, so there!'

The last two juvenile words, so forcefully uttered, brought the day back to its original purpose, and Hassan laughed, his whole countenance alive with amusement. But it became grim again while Mustapha was taking away the dessert plates and setting coffee in their place.

'Thank you, Mustapha,' Alicia told him, thinking that the small amount of alcohol it contained might be a good thing for her metabolism. She took up the small silver spoon and stirred the cream round and round.

The grate of chair-legs on hard-planked boards brought her gaze away from watching swirls of cream beginning to disintegrate. A little astonished, she heard him ask, 'Do you mind if I smoke, Alicia?'

'No, of course not,' she replied, never, however, having seen him smoke before.

He withdrew a black leather case from a pocket and extracted a small dark cheroot. She smiled across, thinking that it suited him.

Returning the smile, he began to speak. 'I have reasons for my attitude, Alicia.'

'Yes, I expect you think you do.' It was with a little astringency that she answered him.

'Yes, well, my father met my mother in England...and fell head over heels in love. She was really very beautiful...'

'Then at least—even if the situation did apply to me, which I know it doesn't—those last few words of yours would rule me out.' Alicia thought that her tone of voice this morning was getting altogether too tart.

'Do they so?' asked Hassan, and the look he directed at her sent—as it had once before—the jolt of a missing heartbeat throughout her whole system.

'"Beautiful" was the word you used. So of course...'

'I did...' Her companion's shoulders went up in a shrug as he continued, 'One has to use words that apply.' Hassan drew on his cheroot, then continued carefully, 'As the story-book says, they got married, but unlike a fairy-tale they didn't live happily ever after.'

'For heaven's sake, Hassan,' Alicia couldn't prevent herself from exclaiming forcefully. 'That happens all the time. With all sorts of people.'

'That may be so. Still, they *were* very much in love, but even so my mother came to hate Egypt. She wanted to go home, she stated, and in the end she did. She had to leave me, of course, because as far as that was concerned she had no option. For I was of the ben Amarna.

'So you see, Alicia,' said a cool, disinterested voice, 'I had an example set before me of what not to do. Oh, don't think I didn't enjoy myself... indulge myself, among the beautiful and charming women available, in Europe, and elsewhere...'

'I wouldn't dream of not thinking that,' a voice which was neither cool nor disinterested interrupted him.

Hassan only laughed, saying, 'I didn't mean to get personal. It was only my way of explaining my attitude. Explaining that, whatever you might think of whatever... it just wouldn't work!'

'By that, do I take it to mean that I am not beautiful enough for you to enjoy yourself with... for you to *indulge* yourself with?' The words were out before she could stop them.

'No, I certainly didn't mean that,' broke in Hassan angrily, sending his cheroot arching high above to fall over the side of the felucca to the water beneath. 'That would be very much to the contrary, I assure you. It does mean, however, that with you I would not risk a future of untold misery and unhappiness.'

Suddenly she didn't care any more. Suddenly she hated this hard, arrogant man—all the warmth of his previous behaviour to her forgotten, lying in ruins about her. She pushed her empty coffee-cup away and sat up straight. And, as if that abrupt movement had set in train the forthcoming course of events, Ali called out.

They were passing Luxor and would soon be at the jetty and home. Home! Her lips twisted bitterly. Well, at the hotel and the safety of her room.

Mustapha was suddenly beside her, handing over to her the big shoulder-bag. She turned, smiling dazzlingly at him, saying, 'Thank you, Mustapha, I have been very pleased to meet you.'

'Thank you, Miss Seacombe, it has also been my pleasure to meet you. Go with Allah!' He had turned, moving away.

Alicia felt quick tears spring to her eyes at the kindness sounding in that voice, but angrily dashed them away. Turning, she saw another face watching her, but quickly lids had fallen to hide any expression, so with her empty camera in one hand, shoulder-bag slung where it belonged, Alicia walked to the edge of the felucca.

At the gangplank, Hassan went to reach for her hand, but sharply she drew back.

'Don't be silly, Alicia,' he told her curtly. 'Watch how you step.'

So she put her hand for the last time into the warm, strong one held out to her, and swung down on to the jetty beside him. She walked along it as she had done a few hours before, if with a different person by her side. She didn't look back!

Ali opened the door of the limousine waiting there, and in a few minutes she was stepping from it before the Winter Palace. She didn't bother to argue again with Ali as he began to escort her towards the entrance. Arriving there, she turned to say thank you politely, manners prevailing, and saw Ali bowing to her. The first time ever. Then he was gone, and she was inside, walking through the large foyer.

A familiar voice calling her name halted her. 'Hi there, my elusive friend,' said Sally.

Alicia smiled hello, decided that her aunt was probably happily engaged reading or resting, so she stayed to talk. 'I thought you were hard at work on some archaeological dig, Sally,' she said.

Sally grasped her arm, words pouring out at her excitably. 'I was...and I will be after tomorrow. However, I've spent the last two days away from it, and because

it was a weekend I was excused. Still, after tomorrow
I'll be back, working even harder.'

'Hey, slow down, and tell me properly what you're
doing here. This hotel is hardly student standard—or
for that matter acting archaeologist's standards, either.'

'No, I know! Isn't it lovely?' Waving an arm around
the opulent foyer, Sally laughed happily, then said,
'Look, you met Charles the other night. Well, I've been
spending the last two days with him, and ... he's taking
me out into the desert tomorrow. I'm so thrilled.'

'Lucky you,' replied Alicia in heartfelt tones, thinking
how much she would like to be going out into the desert
tomorrow also.

'Yes, aren't I just? Charles is here on business, so...
However, come and have a drink with us and say hello.'

Pulled forward willy-nilly, Alicia followed her towards
a group of chairs set round a small coffee-table. She
smiled a greeting then sank down in the seat the man
was pulling out for her, thinking that if she ever thought
of any man again in that context she would say that he
was attractive. Fair, open-faced, beautiful teeth showing
in a happy smile—and, if certainly not carrying the absolute arrogant assurance of another man she knew, he
still had the confidence that wealth and standing brought.

'What are you drinking, Alicia?' and with her reply
he raised a beckoning finger to an attendant.

'You're going out into the desert tomorrow, Sally tells
me,' said Alicia, listening to that girl's excited chatter
about how marvellous Egypt was.

She almost spilt the whole of the newly arrived drink
when Charles replied, 'Yes, I'm going out to buy a
horse—maybe two horses in fact—if one of them lives
up to the reputation which has been flying around about
it.'

Alicia sat immobile, gazing at the waiter as he mopped
up the spilt drink, then said, 'You really are not going

out into the desert to what is called the horse-fair, are
you?'

'Yes, I am, or at least at something called by that
description.' Amazement at the way she had couched
the question coloured the open face. 'How on earth do
you know about such an affair?' he questioned.

'Because...that's where I'd love to be tomorrow. I
have a horse being sold there.'

'You...a young girl...selling a horse there?' If there
had been amazement in that open face before, now there
showed incredulity. Then abruptly he exclaimed, 'Oh,
of course, you're an Australian, and this horse is from
Australia.'

'Yes, I am, and yes, it is. However, I didn't know you
were interested. I did know someone from Vienna was.'

'So I've been informed.' The man across from her
didn't seem so open-faced now. Gazing at her was a hard
business countenance.

'I don't think it really matters, because I have been
informed that I have no need to be concerned. That he
will be sold, even with the reserve which has been placed
upon him; and it is a very high reserve,' finished Alicia
carefully. But, thinking of the source of that information, she couldn't prevent a hard core of bitterness
sounding.

'Oh, and what would that amount be?'

Alicia laughed at him.

Charles had the grace to smile back. 'Is he as good
as I've been told? Because I did have every intention of
buying two Arabs, one for my sister and one for myself.
Now...I don't know! We are well known equestrians,
you know.'

'I didn't know. I've only ridden in Queensland.
However, not on Dark Shadow. He's too young. Still,
he has been trained, and he's so beautiful... I only wish
I could ride him and show you.'

'Why can't you? You could go and see him sold. Show him off.'

'I only wish I could. But I've been forbidden to go.'

'Forbidden?'

'Oh, yes. They don't like women going there.'

'Well, tomorrow they will find that their wishes don't always apply, because Sally is coming with me.'

'Are you really going there, Sally? I didn't . . . I was informed that women didn't go to it.'

'Tough cheese for them. I'm a buyer, and I'm taking Sally. I already have our tickets for the helicopter, and she's thrilled to be going with me. Aren't you, my sweet?'

'It will be the icing on the cake for these last two days, Charles. You know I've been thrilled with them too,' replied the irrepressible Sally.

Alicia sat there, wondering . . .

CHAPTER EIGHT

EVEN with the throb of sound all about her, Alicia knew that it was not a trip in a noisy helicopter which was the cause of the sinking, apprehensive feeling in her stomach. Remembering the arrogant, decisive man who had declared so particularly that a horse auction was no place for a woman, she made every endeavour to force her thoughts away from the past two days—and the man whose presence had coloured both of them.

Having no window to look from, she glanced over at the pilot—an Egyptian—wondering what his feelings and attitude would be if he knew ... But he didn't know, so it didn't matter. He had handed over a ticket in exchange for traveller's cheques, quite happy to do so when Charles had approached him.

Alicia had clutched the piece of paper in a damp palm, then zipped the other piece down carefully into a side pocket of her bag. Charles had laughed at her on seeing the care with which she treated both tickets.

'For heaven's sake, Alicia,' he had told her almost sharply, 'The world of today doesn't belong in the deep dark past. This auction you are going to is a recognised affair wherever horses are spoken of, or ridden. Why all this worry and heartache?' He had sounded half contemptuous. After all, wasn't he, Charles, taking her? And Charles had no false modesty as to who he was.

Nevertheless, she knew she was going to hang on to Sally very tightly. Because Charles didn't know Hassan, or the power he wielded. Still, Hassan wouldn't be there; he would be out in the far desert somewhere.

102

Now, observing Sally laughing across at her, and realising that her expression could be showing the thoughts chasing one another through her mind, she smiled suddenly. Charles was right. She was stupid to be worrying. Then ... those tiny fingers of unease were playing havoc once again throughout her entire being. They were going down.

So, taking the usual deeply needed breath, she unstrapped herself and was helped down—on to Hassan's home ground. She saw she was on a dark helicopter pad set amid sand dunes extending in every direction—except one.

Charles's words came to her as the noise of the rotors stopped. 'Over there, I expect. I wonder...' He stopped speaking as something like a jeep, but with great big bulbous tyres, came roaring towards them. They all climbed into it. As their strange vehicle got closer, Alicia saw that all the activity seemed around one oasis—a small one, entirely separated from a very large one further across. There was a large roped ring with a horse in it being auctioned.

They were set down and a hand pointed. Moving across to where it gestured, they found themselves beside a cluster of Europeans spread out under the shade of waving palm fronds. Apparently Arabs didn't need shade, because they were there, but out in the open in small groups together.

This seemed to be all right, thought Alicia hopefully, but her hand still held tightly on to Sally's. Then her heartbeat stilled for a moment. Over on the far edge beside a beaten path extending between the two oases stood a small group. She recognised the colours.

Her attention was brought back to her own affairs when Charles said, 'This is Herr Werder, Sally, from Vienna, whom I have met in equestrian events; and this, Herr Werder, is Alicia Seacombe from Australia.'

'Australia, eh? You appear to be well represented,' smiled the charming elderly man, then continued, 'There are more of your countrymen here. But those we have to worry about are the Arabs. Oh...' He broke off, turning as the auctioneer came to stand beside them. 'You know one another?' he asked.

'Yes indeed!' The newcomer had a greeting for Charles, a small bow when Sally was introduced, and the barest inclination of the head for Alicia. It was returned in kind. She shrugged; what did it matter as long as Dark Shadow was sold?

He told them, and he did include her with almost the smile he had given to her yesterday, 'Look, the morning's selling is finished. Refreshments will be brought out to you, and we are resuming at one-thirty.'

So beside Sally, who was sitting close to Charles, Alicia drank tea, but refused eatables, and later, remembering this day, she remembered it as passing in a haze. She found it incredible that every animal had to be looked at and examined. Her male companion behaving as badly as the rest. And in between, in the distance of her mind, she heard the helicopters come and go.

The day passed, blazingly hot under a wide-arched sky of deep indigo. Still, giving them a semblance of coolness, came a breeze which caught and sent the palm fronds above stirring.

Then from out of the haziness which encompassed her she heard words that did break through. And into that ring before her, jumping and pulling upon a leading rein, came a horse. A murmur of sound echoed from around her. He *had* been looked after, she noticed with the one glance she got, for he was abruptly hidden from her. Waiting back carefully, then unable to prevent herself, she moved forward as the selling ring emptied.

'Shadow, darling,' she called softly, and the beautiful shining black horse turned. He looked at her, then, taking a step forward as she hurried across, still speaking softly, he greeted her. Her attention on only one subject, she didn't even hear another concerted murmur echoing from so many different throats.

Her arm around a satiny neck, she nuzzled her face into his shoulder, giving him the cubes of sugar as payment for his reception of her. Then, becoming aware of her surroundings, she gave a last stroke, a last pat, and walked back to her place. If there were tears in her eyes, she scrubbed them firmly away with her wrist. There was no way she could manage to keep him.

Unaware of what Mr Aziz was calling out, a gasp from Sally brought her attention back... 'So we will start the bidding at forty thousand dollars.'

For a long minute no one did start, then a nod came. And so it went on. At her reserve, she wheeled on Charles, saying, 'Don't go on, it's getting too high.'

He gazed at her without the slightest sign of recognition, then raised a finger. One minute later, she felt the tense body beside her relax as a small cry of triumph issued.

'Well, he's not yours any longer, Alicia. He's mine,' he told her.

'He was very expensive,' she said carefully.

'He could have been twice as expensive and I would have bought him. I think I got him cheap,' and, reaching out, he clasped her close to bend down and kiss her thoroughly. She tried to prevent it. She couldn't, and stood there before a crowd of men, embraced thoroughly, kissed thoroughly.

Freed, she put up a hand to rub across smarting lips. However, Charles wasn't interested in her now. He never had been; that little exhibition had occurred because he had been thrilled to get what he wanted. He was over now, patting his horse. Then the auctioneer was beside him, leading him towards his table.

Alicia gazed round apprehensively. Some men were looking her way. Some—the European contingent half smiling, others blank-faced. Then, as she swung her gaze around as if drawn by a magnet, she saw the ben Amarna group. 'Great heavens!' she gasped as she looked directly at a fierce-looking old man with, of all people, Yusef standing a pace behind. He saw her too, she knew. He gave no sign that he had.

Sally was speaking excitedly to her, 'Yes, I know it is,' she replied. 'But the money isn't all mine. Still, thank you, Sally darling, for enabling me to come. I will always remember Dark Shadow as he is now.' She broke off as Sally ran to throw herself into a returning Charles's arms.

She thought, great Scott, the natives are getting an eyefull today, but the ben Amarna group had already departed, thank goodness.

She stood by herself, not wanting to break in upon Sally and Charles, but aware suddenly of Sally's angry voice. 'It can't be helped, my sweet,' Charles was telling her as he came across to where Alicia was standing. 'Look, Alicia, you tell her that I have to go. They are taking the sold horses halfway to Luxor, resting them for a few hours, then journeying on before the heat of the next midday. There's no way I am flying back in a helicopter and leaving this horse I have just bought. I'm even flying with him on the plane home. Tell her, Alicia, that I've got to!'

Even though commiserating with Sally, she knew she would do the same. However, Charles was interrupting. 'Look,' he was saying as he gazed down at the sullen face, 'I have something I was keeping to give you tomorrow, but come along over to my pack now.'

He went with his arm around her, and unhappily Alicia stood there, alone. She knew she couldn't follow them. Her reverie was interrupted by a voice at her elbow. 'I'll escort you to the helicopter, Miss Seacombe,' said Yusef.

Unaware of his even being in her vicinity, never mind accosting her, she almost stammered. 'I...I'm waiting for someone.'

'The arrangements have all been changed, so you had better come now or you will miss your seat.' He didn't act like the young Sheikh Yusef she had met only yesterday morning. If she closed her eyes it could have been Hassan speaking in his most autocratic way. She didn't know what to do. Sally and Charles were still some way off. But yes, she knew arrangements had been changed.

A sharp, impatient voice spoke. 'If you want to obtain a seat, you had better come now. I am going!'

She went. She did want to get away from here now. And, after all, nothing could happen to her on the way to the helicopter. Also, after all, this was Yusef, a paramount sheikh of the ben Amarna. So she walked the few yards then stepped into the strange vehicle. Out of it and beside one of the helicopters with engines already started, she was piloted inside.

Indicated to take one of the vacant seats, she hesitated, trying to look out for Sally. The other two passengers, one a woman, the other in familiar colours, didn't speak.

The outside door slammed. The rotors were like thunder, and then they were off. She had a window this time and could look down, far down upon what looked like a busy ant-heap, horses and people all mixed up and scurrying around. Then the 'copter banked and turned, and all she could see were the towering palms of the large oasis.

What would Sally think of her, going off like this? Still, looking back, there had been nothing else she could have done. Yusef was Yusef, and... She glanced at her two fellow passengers. Neither was looking at her, and of course the pilot was gazing where he should: at his instrument panel.

The journey seemed to go on for longer than the
outward one from Luxor had seemed to do. But
eventually, when the sun was almost at the horizon,
Alicia saw they were going down. Suddenly she was apprehensive. This place to where they were descending
was not Luxor. This was the middle of the desert. The
other two passengers moved past her to disembark. The
pilot looked round, motioning her to do the same.

What would happen if she just stayed there in her seat?
But she knew she couldn't, not knowing where she might
end up. Also, Yusef had put her on this helicopter. He,
like Hassan, with all he was and all he owned, would
have no need to abduct his women. So, unfastening
straps, she walked straight back to the open door—and
jumped. Almost immediately, the rotors quickened their
pace and the machine was rising above her. Alicia felt
abandoned as she watched it rise then turn and grow
smaller.

Her glance went to her companions, but they were
looking towards the only landmark to break the sym-
metry of the rolling sand dunes. From a few lone palms
came some moving dots. As she watched, Alicia thought
she could be seeing a picture from out of the Bible—or
even from a time before that.

Caught in the blaze of a setting sun, with the desert
all about them turning from sepia, to dark brown, to
cinnamon, the five pale camels paced towards them, and
Alicia saw that only two of the beasts held riders.

From somewhere far within her came words she had
heard spoken in a hospital corridor. A crisp voice saying,
'If you are associating me with any thoughts of a white
slave trade, I beg leave to tell you that in these permissive days I hardly think it is still a flourishing
business. Even if it were, allow me to inform you...'

But that voice had enamated from Hassan. It was
Yusef who had sent her on *this* journey. She told herself

abruptly not to be silly. Yusef was only about her own
age; there was nothing to be frightened of about him.
So why was she? Because remembering those fierce hawklike eyes, remembering his own kind of absolute assurance and demand which told its own story, she knew
that she was. Endeavouring to take no notice of the
tightening knot of apprehension as she watched those
moving dots come closer, she swallowed from a nervous
throat, then turned to the woman beside her.

She asked, without even hoping she would understand, 'Could you tell me please where we are going?'

And heard with unutterable relief the answer coming
to her in English. Accented English certainly, but quite
fluent. For a startled moment she didn't take in the
woman's words, just the language. Then they hit out at
her.

'We are going to the lord Hassan's oasis.'

The lord Hassan. Alicia couldn't believe it. Then that
knot of apprehension within her turned to anger. Why
go to the trouble of all this charade? Why not just arrange for her to take the journey properly? Then the
twist of tension deep inside reasserted itself as she remembered his almost last words to her. 'It does mean,
however, that with you I would not risk a future of
untold misery and unhappiness.' So what had changed
that attitude? Changing his mind was certainly not
Hassan's way. Why...? And what about Aunt Em? she
thought, angry again. Aunt Em would be frantic.

The camels came to a halt before their three figures,
and the woman, turning to Alicia, said, 'I am called
Soraya. We are to go now.'

What was she to do? Of course she had to mount one
of the damned things. She was told with a smile. 'Look,
like this. But first you are to take this, as it will get cold
later.' Being handed a folded white cloak, Alicia took it
absently for it was still hot—when suddenly she was

transported to a night in Cairo. She had thought then that the aroma of sandalwood would always bring to her the memory of Hassan. Did this cloak belong to him, or had it just been folded in a sandalwood chest?

So, with no option, she stepped on to the crouching camel, just as she had been ordered, and was almost immediately high up in the air. They set off, she and her two travelling companions in the centre, the two new-comers on either side. They carried long, lethal-looking rifles across their shoulders.

Even with anger still burning inside her at the cavalier way she had been—and whichever way you looked at it, the word was 'kidnapped'—Alicia couldn't prevent the incredible beauty of the undulating sand dunes through which they were riding colour her mind. With the sun almost below the horizon now, its searching rays still gave shades of difference to the configuration of the sands—first on one side then on the other. It was pure magic.

Her leg curled round the horn of the saddle, Alicia held firmly to the reins, and found that it wasn't as un-comfortable as she had expected. The haughty beast carried her along like a horse in a fast canter.

The desert was all about them now, only the sound of the swiftly padding hooves cushioned by soft sand and the creak of saddle-leather broke the hush in which they moved.

Finding she could manage to stay on quite well, Alicia now had time to look about her. There was no moon, but a luminosity outlined the shape of the riders grouped closely around her, and, gazing upwards, she saw the stars scintillating as if a lavish hand had scattered blazing diamonds upon a black velvet canopy. It was the bril-liance of these which provided the faint brightness.

Alicia drew in a deep breath. No matter the way she had been brought to this pass . . . no matter why, it was

exhilarating to be riding through this vast silence, a
breeze coming from no one knew where, sending her
hair flying back from her face.

Still, she wondered a little later on how much longer
they would be riding, feeling as if they had been flying
through this night forever. Also feeling much colder now,
she shifted carefully in the saddle to bring the warm
fleecy cloak more closely around herself.

Then suddenly, in the faint starshine, a smudge on the
horizon came to mar the emptiness about them. Also
suddenly, there came a blink of light. Could a star be
that low down? Then another brighter glint showed, and
in a few minutes they were among palm trees and there
were men coming to meet them . . . and the civilisation
of large tents.

A bearded man was beside her camel, and it went
grunting to the ground. She looked round for Hassan.
He wasn't there!

She found she had to lean back against the shoulder
of the kneeling camel for a moment, legs cramped from
the long ride, body shaking with cold.

'Through here, lady,' said Soraya, gesturing.

Alicia went through and stood gazing about her. Well,
there was one thing, she thought: this place, like his other
quarters, wasn't the setting for some *Arabian Nights*
scenario. A thick carpet did cover the floor upon which
she stood, but around her the furniture and décor were
that of a working man's room.

It was lit by electric light.

'Through here, lady,' Soraya said again. This time,
however, she was indicating a wide opening.

'No, I'm not going through there. Where is the lord
Hassan? You said this place belonged to him, so where
is he?' Yusef had sent her, so could——?

Her thoughts were interrupted, 'Oh, yes, lady. This place is called the Far Oasis. It belongs to the lord Hassan,' replied Soraya happily.

'Well, where is he?' Alicia was not really frightened . . . yet. This Far Oasis or whatever undoubtedly did belong to Hassan; but she *was* getting sick with nerves. She couldn't understand what was happening.

'He is delayed. He will come soon,' the woman was saying, then was adding, 'The lord Hassan says for you to bathe and change. He will be here to eat with you.'

'I am not going to bathe and change. What would I change into? I don't even want to stay.' Alicia went to walk to the outside opening, taking no notice of Soraya's upset cry behind her. There was a man standing there, a guard with a rifle down by his side.

'Please, lady, you are to do as the lord Hassan says. He is very angry. And we all obey him quickly when he is like that. I have never seen him so angry,' replied Soraya.

'I don't care if he is angry,' Alicia was beginning, and then thought, Yes, I do. So she walked hesitantly through the held-back flap.

She found herself pushed gently into a chair, with the ankle-length boots being pulled off.

'No, I can manage,' she half laughed then, fending Soraya off as she began to help with the rest of her clothes.

The bathroom when she went through a thick curtain almost made her stop being so angry and smile. It certainly wasn't like Hassan's harem quarters at Luxor, but it was concreted and there was a shower.

Standing under the cold, streaming water, for one short moment she allowed it to wash away the traumatic tensions that this day had provided—but it was only for a moment. The towel Soraya was waiting to hand her reminded her of Hassan: pristine white, and having the aroma of sandalwood. Soraya was also handing out to her a long white garment.

'No,' she said. Her body dried, she was rubbing at the ends of wet hair as she went back into the big tented room. 'I'll put my own clothes back on, dirt and all.'

'No, lady, they have been sent out to wash. You are to wear this, the lord Hassan said.' Frightened or not, Alicia was getting tired of the very sound of the lord Hassan, and shook her head.

'You must, lady... please.' The thin muslin gown was being held out to her once again.

What else could she do? She couldn't stand here naked. So she slipped her arms through loose sleeves, and the gown, like an old-fashioned kimono, fell open all the way down. It could, of course, wrap round her twice over.

Soraya glanced at her for a moment, then went to a tall sandalwood press, returning with something that was familiar. Pulling the much too large garment around Alicia, she bound it firmly about the waist with the maroon and white cord she had extracted from it—then smiled a little anxiously at the other woman.

Still rubbing absently at hair now beginning to dry, Alicia pushed away the comb being handed to her, saying, 'No, I have my own,' and rummaged through the large shoulder-bag. At least, she thought, she still had this with all its contents, so, withdrawing the comb, she decided quite dispassionately to ignore any of the make-up it contained. She had been made to dress as she was by that arrogant man's orders. She would certainly not try to make herself attractive for him.

Hair combed straight, gown gathered up around her waist, she decided that it was so enveloping it didn't show too much of her outline. She walked firmly into the other room. She glanced over the books stacked on some shelves at the far end. Engineering treatises mostly, the others written in Arabic.

Moving restlessly about, Alicia wondered about this affair, this bizarre turning her life had taken. Why? Hassan had said so definitely that they were finished. And . . . Hassan always only said what he meant. Surely this—abduction—wasn't because she had defied him and gone to the horse-fair. If she was nothing to him he should have simply ignored her behaviour, and shrugged his shoulders at the whole affair.

Anyhow, would he have known? He should have been here—in the far desert, as he had told her he would be. Again she moved restlessly up and down, her footsteps making no sound on the thick carpet.

Then, like only the faintest vibration of the air, she heard a sound, and then came the noise of hurried bustling, of voices calling loudly, of quick movement at some distance. She moved to the side of the outside opening. The guard hadn't moved. He was still there. If anything he seemed to be standing even straighter.

The noise was becoming louder. It *was* a helicopter. But not one of the sort she had travelled in twice today. This sound roared all about them. It must be huge. She glanced over at Soraya.

'It is a big military helicopter, to go long distances, and is bringing the lord Hassan,' said her companion.

Suddenly she couldn't even think. The roar was encompassing the entire world, then it dimmed a little. For the space of seconds it remained that way, then the enormous sound was all about them once again, as, rising to depart, the machine flew off about its own business once more.

Abruptly she was sick with apprehension, and then tried to unclench the fists which had fastened into knots at her side. This was Hassan, she told herself, who had shown her love...kindness...and a side of Egypt she would always remember.

How could she be so silly...so frightened?

CHAPTER NINE

WORDS echoed from outside, harsh Arabic words, and Alicia heard the sound of someone departing. Oh, of course, she thought sardonically, the guard was not needed now. The lord and master of all this entire place was home.

And then he had entered, a figure dressed in the same clothes like the ones she had seen him in at a hospital in Cairo. He stood just inside, making only one gesture, and Soraya slipped from the tent. He made another and unhooked the tent flap, allowing it to fall solidly into place.

All her worry and apprehension departed happily away. This was Hassan, and she ran forward to meet him. She stopped abruptly, unable to finish her little rush as she saw his face now as the light fell upon it.

He was reaching up to pull off his kaffiyeh, to throw it on to the small table beside the couch. He remained motionless for another long moment, then lifted a hand to put a small cheroot to his mouth.

Apprehension flooding back, Alicia looked at him— at a different man from the one she had previously known. 'What is it, Hassan—what is this affair all about?' she couldn't prevent herself from asking.

The man moved a pace forward, and a long brown finger reached out to flick the white muslin open. 'Very nice too,' said a strange, soft voice. 'Dressed as you should be, to entertain a visitor.'

Feeling the scorching touch that finger had left upon her bare breast, Alicia took a sharp step backwards. She

116

went to speak, then tried again as no words issued. 'What is the matter? Why are you behaving like this? And why…bring me out here without even asking…or telling me about it.'

'I simply had no time to worry about what convention dictates. I had other important affairs on my mind. However, I don't have to worry about those now. I was quite free, and I am here—we are both here, so we can enjoy the rest of the night. And also the next four or five days. I think that might be enough!'

She heard those arrogant words. She heard the hardness behind them. She wasn't a schoolroom miss. This was today's world and she knew what he meant when speaking them.

Her back straightened and her chin went up. She said only one word. 'Why?'

'But surely you would know why? As other men do, I like to indulge myself occasionally, so I intend to enjoy these next few hours…these next few days.'

Casting her mind back to wonder what could have brought this on, to cause him to become so antagonistic towards her, she tried to think. She knew he had had no need to do this thing. She knew what could have happened in Luxor if Yusef's phone call had not come. He, of course, man of the world that he was, would have known it also. She said again, 'Why?'

'I think I have already told you why, and I am getting a little tired of being asked.' He moved another step forward, and that finger again parted the thin muslin; but this time it went much lower. This time, though, she stepped back and dragged the material together. He laughed, a sound coming deep within his throat.

'No, you haven't told me why!' Unclenching teeth which had been shut tight, she went on sarcastically, 'Surely the great Sheikh Hassan ben Amarna has no need to abduct his women. I would once have thought otherwise.'

'No, the great Sheikh Hassan ben Amarna has no need to behave like that—as you probably know from your own experience.' His words stopped, but she knew what they had been suggesting. Then, seeing his glance rove completely over her, from cheeks coloured now in scarlet flame that a surging memory brought to them, she threw up a hand in defence. A low laugh again from deep within his throat was all that answered her.

'However,' that unfamiliar soft, silken voice was continuing, 'when someone I have known, and been seen with, and have tried to protect, behaves as you did today, I can certainly drop even the thought of being chivalrous. Especially when I am a paramount sheikh of the ben Amarna and my actions were known . . . and public.'

'Public . . .' Contempt echoed in the word. 'Who would know? Who would care?'

'Oh, people would know, believe me. In the East, words and actions fly like a forest fire. They would know, my little promiscuous houri, that I walked out of that hospital with you, called for you and took you to Karnak, and spent a whole day with you on one of our feluccas. Oh, yes, all Egypt would know.'

Gazing at the face opposite as those words burnt into her consciousness, Alicia thought it must be the uncertain light which made it appear as it did—like some graven image from another time, granite-hard, frightening.

'For everyone—the paramount sheikh of my people included—to see you embraced, and kissed, by a man in an open public arena——' The words came across to her as if dredged from molten flame . . . they were interrupted before they could be continued.

'You should train your spies more thoroughly! Instruct them to see things in context,' she was beginning, when in her turn she was interrupted.

'It wasn't what you term "my spies". If they had witnessed such a scandalous event, they would never have dared to speak of it to me—they would have been too frightened. I saw it myself... and it was as well that I could do nothing about it then. But now... oh, now it is a different matter altogether.'

'I didn't... I didn't...' She was beginning to defend herself when a sharp chopping motion with a decisive hand silenced her.

'I don't want to hear. I don't even want to know what you paid him... how you paid him to bring you...' She went to raise a hand as if to hit him. She let it fall when the soft, silken voice said, 'I wouldn't...I really wouldn't if I were you.'

However, he was continuing. 'As I have all the time in the world before me, I think I would prefer to have dinner first. I have not eaten all day.'

Whose fault was that? she would have liked to ask, but didn't dare. She did dare to ask, though, 'What about my aunt? She will be frantic when I don't arrive back.'

'She has been informed,' was all the answer she received.

'Has she, indeed? Just like that! I simply can't believe this behaviour of yours.'

'Oh, believe it! As I have said once before, you are going to have some few days to believe it.' He walked over and, hooking back the tent flap, called.

Mustapha must have been waiting; he entered with a laden tray.

Alicia glanced at this man she had liked, and incredibly, seeing where they were, and what had occurred, heard him say gently, 'Good evening, Miss

Seacombe.' She also saw the black scowl which came to sit between two drawn together brows.

He stalked to the entrance and sent his cheroot arching into the night. He then indicated a chair as Mustapha left. He didn't walk round to seat her. As she still remained at the other end of the room, he told her with the silken softness turning into a drawling slur which frightened her more than anything else had done, 'I told you, I wouldn't mind eating first, but it is immaterial to me what we do.'

This time he indicated the opening into the back room. She went and sat down! She drank the soup, but when Mustapha put a main course before her she knew she would not be able to swallow.

She looked up almost imploringly at him as he glanced up from his plate, and said, 'I didn't expect what happened when Dark Shadow was sold; it was just...'

'Don't tell me what was just... You were forbidden to go. Yet you did, and ended up causing every male there to have his own thoughts about you.'

'They must have little else to think about, then.' Suddenly Alicia was angry too, and she went on, 'And if it is finished between us, why did you bother? Why not let me go home, back to Luxor and out of your life?'

'Oh, I decided it was better finished when I thought of you as I did then. Now—oh, now, knowing so differently, I will add to that attraction we once had and show you what a different kind of lovemaking is all about!'

'Oh, yes, of course you can. When you have your cousin—and your uncle too for all I know—to help in your abductions. Of course you can—what was it you told me once?—indulge yourself——' She stopped speaking abruptly as if the words had been cut off by a slicing knife. She hadn't been prepared for the violent anger that made his chair go flying back, overturned. She wasn't prepared, either, for the blazing fire that shone from those emerald eyes—or for the words issuing from lips thinned to a cruel white line.

'Don't dare mention my family. Do you think I enjoyed that scene—do you think I was overjoyed at seeing how wrong my judgement had been? Well...we'll see what this new judgement of mine is going to bring to fruition.'

He walked round the table and, really frightened now, as if she was participating in some nightmare, Alicia pushed back her chair also, and stood.

She found she was being pushed before him into the other room, which in its turn had its flap untied and dropped to the floor. They stood together, confined in a closeness of dimly lit space.

He moved a step nearer, his head coming down. A voice, slurred and unfamiliar, said, 'You won't mind, Alicia, will you, if I don't use the care and gentleness I would have once done when making love to you? I have decided that that is not necessary. So tonight...now I can allow all my need, my desire to take whatever course it finds its way along.'

Panicking, understanding those offensive words flung at her, Alicia opened her mouth to protest. All and every objection was smothered as his lips came down upon her own, caressing them with slow kisses which brought their own response. After all, this was Hassan. The bronzed, classical face from another era lifted, and from deep within his throat Hassan laughed mockingly as he said, 'Do you respond to all your lovers so satisfyingly with the first kiss?' And, picking her up, he swung her upon the turned-down bed.

With the heavy body so close along her side, one arm crushed beneath her, the other held loosely by a strong brown hand, all she could see was his head downbent, gazing intently at what his fingers were doing.

He then said, 'I didn't know this thing had other uses as well as adorning my kaffiyeh, but it has served its purpose here as it does there.' The maroon and white cord was now completely unfastened and thrown carelessly aside. One long finger moved slowly and set apart the soft white muslin, then travelled down the bare silken skin that it had exposed.

Alicia's eyes closed, but she took a deep breath and, her voice tight, told him with as much contempt as she could muster colouring her words, 'I can't stop anything you propose to do. How can I? But it will be you alone doing any lovemaking that occurs. And I will hate you forever afterwards.'

The slurred voice, holding strain far back, only answered carelessly, 'Who will care if you hate me forever afterwards? When these few days are gone, there will be no afterwards. But for now...' His lips resting upon her temple, began travelling along her bare exposed throat, stopping once to cover a pulse that jumped...remaining on it...caressing it...

Then, with his lips raised for a moment, she heard him laugh before they went on their travels again. They stopped next to wander crossways back and forth, taking no notice as she tried to twist away a body clamped tight. Then, as if sending the world about them sliding into oblivion, as if allowing desire and unrestricted passion to colour the entire atmosphere around their two entwined figures, Hassan's lovemaking changed.

The arm spreadeagled beneath her pulled her yet closer, bringing flesh to meet flesh, curves melting into hollows, while his hand stroked down over a half-covered breast, a muslin-covered hip, then trailed oh, so slowly up again.

Suddenly, his mouth came seeking urgently, and she knew with distress that they had passed the point of no return. Tears she had resolutely held back trailed down her cheeks, tears of regret for what could have been. Hassan's searching lips were hard now, demanding, crushing away thought and reason, so that without her volition those burning caresses were carrying her along with him—regrets, thoughts, everything gone with the wind.

Then ... so alarmingly, so unexpectedly, Hassan lifted lips from the throat he was caressing, one arm still clasping her body stretched tightly into his, the other resting on a bare midriff. It was this one which was lifted to wipe against his mouth.

'Allah...' It was in Arabic, that violent expletive came, then, with an abrupt, sharp movement, Hassan had risen to glance down at that supine figure beneath him. Then he was up off the bed and, reaching out, had suddenly switched on a lamp standing on a night table. Curled up in the middle of the rumpled bedclothes, Alicia threw up a hand to shield her eyes.

'Yes, it is strong. It is my reading lamp.'

As if those mundane words had broken through to the girl lying there, she scrambled up to stand on the far side of the bed, trying to bring the sides of the thin muslin together about her.

Across the yards separating them, they looked at one another, then the man said in a voice still strained and husky, 'Well, Alicia, this I have to say: you have accomplished something no other woman has done before. For I tell you that in all my affairs throughout my long years I have never had to hold in my arms—or make love to—a woman in tears. They brought me to my senses.'

'I am not crying... I am not!' she said sharply, but she was gazing at him through tear-drenched eyes.

'You don't know how lucky you are,' said that still unfamiliar voice. 'If I hadn't had to take an important visitor back to Luxor, and attend a formal affair, I would have taken you from that fair to my quarters at the oasis, and nothing would have stopped me then—not even tears. To see you...' Hassan's hand went down in a sharp cutting movement.

'I didn't know it was going to happen...' she was beginning. 'I didn't know...I'm sorry. I'm not...' she made herself say it. 'I'm not a promiscuous houri.'

A lopsided smile came to part those sculptured lips before her. 'Did I call you that? You got off lightly. You just don't know!'

'Very well, I will apologise for going to the fair. You were right. I shouldn't have gone! So now could I have my clothes please, and...?' She stopped suddenly, realising how stupid it was to ask to be taken home, from this far place, in the middle of the night.

His head turned sharply and, in the brief sideways glance she caught, Alicia saw a different smile part those lips. She drew in a deep, relieved breath, however. She could manage him if he was smiling; then the words she was thinking surfaced through her consciousness, and she told herself forcefully not to be stupid yet again. Of course she couldn't manage him; that had been entirely the wrong word—but she could certainly be less apprehensive.

Then a puzzled frown came to twist her brows. What was he doing, rummaging in the bed among the rumpled covers. She decided with more than a little astringency that he couldn't be trying to remake it. She wouldn't imagine, remembering his behaviour and conversation from the last two days, that he had ever made a bed, or would even know how it was done.

He was turning towards her, the bed and its disarranged covering still as they had been. He said, 'Perhaps this might come in handy,' holding out towards her the maroon and white cord. There was no smile upon his countenance this time; it showed only the normal face he presented to the world. If there was any expression lurking behind those magnetic eyes, it didn't show.

However, the memory of what that cord had been used for, and of how that purpose had been utterly disposed of, brought a warm, staining scarlet to colour her cheeks.

From somewhere deep inside her she vowed that when she had left this place, when this man before her had gone out of her life, when she got home, she was never going to blush again. However, now she replied only with studied politeness, 'Yes, thank you, I will be pleased to have it.'

He didn't come towards her, just held out a hand with, dangling from it, the cord normally used for binding his kaffiyeh.

The girl only moved one pace forward, and, reaching out a hand, took hold of it as it hung straight down. Fingers released their clasp. Turning a little sideways, Alicia pulled the voluminous garment firmly about her, then tied the cord tightly.

Hassan said then in a natural, conversational tone, 'Now, how about finishing that dinner which was interrupted?'

Alicia looked at him, aghast. She didn't want to eat. She certainly didn't want to go out into that other room, and look at the half-used dishes and pushed-back up-ended chairs.

She said, her voice unsteady, going high, 'I am not hungry. I don't want to eat, and...' Alicia broke off, wondering what Mustapha, what the other servants would think. The thought made her cringe. She said again, 'I don't want any dinner.'

'Well, I do. I haven't eaten at all today, and...'

'You can't go out there and have that food removed and order fresh... You can't!'

'Can I not?' One eyebrow had risen alarmingly. The voice that replied, sounded as if grating on silk.

'What will Mustapha think? What will the others...?'

'My people, Alicia,' interrupted the voice in that same tone, 'don't think about what I do. They don't talk about what I do. They only always obey orders I give... and swiftly, too. Now...' Hassan stood back and indicated the aperture through which she had been pushed so roughly just a little time ago.

She went, the man standing well back so as not to crowd her. In the living-room she had her first surprise. The overturned chair had been set upright, the dishes taken away, the table reset and looking pristine fresh. She shook her head.

Hassan moved past her and at the still open entrance called softly. Returning, he held her chair for her. Perforce, she sat down.

Her companion moved first to the desk, to take up a large manilla envelope resting at its edge. He carried it to the table and asked politely, 'Will you excuse me, Alicia? This was brought in by military helicopter, and might be important.'

Then Mustapha was there and Hassan was speaking sharply to him in swift Arabic. He received back a nod and, departing, Mustapha smiled at her before leaving.

Alicia didn't smile back—or speak.

Almost at once he was back to set sandwiches before them. They must have been already prepared, thought Alicia, gazing at the delicate triangles upon her plate. Feeling herself being watched, she glanced up. Across the table from her a green fire of emerald showed glinting streaks of reflected light. She was sure it also showed laughter within it, and wondered furiously how he could be so light-hearted after all the trauma this dreadful night had provided.

A hand went up suddenly, palm outward. 'Sorry, Alicia,' he told her, 'but what you were thinking was written all over your face. This situation——' his hand went out in a throwaway gesture to the room all about them '—is not one that occurs here regularly—despite sandwiches being already prepared. I often call for them at night after working on problems. In fact, this circumstance has never occurred here before at all...'

'Oh, does that word "here" mean it could have happened at other localities? After all, with all the manpower; the different methods of transport you have at your fingertips, why not?' She could be angry too—and show it, she decided.

'You are turning into a proper little vixen, aren't you?' said what was now an even, pleasant voice. 'Drink your tea.'

Mustapha was beside her, pouring tea from a pot into a large breakfast cup. He placed the milky liquid beside her plate with sugar basin close beside it. Alicia used the small spoon and stirred, then, lifting the cup in both hands, she drank. The flavour was a little different from that which she normally drank. But of course this wasn't Australian tea; it probably came from India. It was still how she liked it, piping hot and strong. She drank, then, setting the cup back into its saucer, picked up a sandwich. She found she could eat it.

Glancing across the table, she saw that her companion was engaged in his papers. She felt herself yawning. Still, it had been a long day.

She didn't see Hassan rise and come round to her, and stand immobile for a long minute. Then he had swept her up in his arms to carry her through the looped-back opening. There she was lowered upon the bed and, head bowed, bending over her, he became busy with his hands.

But it took only seconds to untie the knot which had only minutes before been tied so tightly. The cord which normally bound his kaffiyeh lay loosely now among the crumpled bedclothes. He pulled up a sheet and tucked it around her, then reached to extinguish the light. The small one Soraya had kindled, he left—a tiny wick in a bowl of oil which had been used down the years from when the Pharaohs had ruled this country. He left the room.

The table was cleared and Mustapha was standing beside the desk, holding in one hand a large cup from which steam was rising, the unfinished sandwiches in the other. Hassan touched his shoulder as he walked past. He sat, and pulled the radio towards him. While he was waiting he drank his tea and ate, then began to speak in sharp, official tones. For a few minutes he spoke, then waited, listening, before switching off.

Seeing Mustapha still waiting, looking at him, he gave a lopsided smile and said, 'I'd better, I suppose.' So once again he spoke, in a different tone, however. He listened, then, with his voice sharpening, he spoke one harsh, quick sentence, and flipped a switch.

'Not tomorrow, then?' asked Mustapha.

'No!' was the one word he received in reply.

Mustapha went to speak again, but after a glance at his companion's scowling face he remained silent, turning away. He dropped shut the flap of the tent entrance and left.

Hassan lay down, his arm going over a face buried in the pillow. Then the faint noise which had been with them all evening went quiet as a generator was switched off. Only silence reigned all about them now, both outside and inside the large tent.

CHAPTER TEN

A RAY of sunshine crept along the floor, finding its way across one room and then the other to slide up and begin playing hide and seek about a supine figure lying on the large bed. An arm was thrown up to push the warmth of it away, and Alicia turned over to curl up again. Aunt Em couldn't be up yet, she thought hazily. There was no sound coming from the kitchen.

But as she turned, a whiff of alien perfume was wafted up to her and abruptly she was awake and leaning up on an elbow. Sandalwood... of course. The room about her was dim, only the wide opening allowing in the sunlight. She looked down at herself; at the sheet tucked around her, at the muslin gown twisted every which way. Her searching hand found the cord that had tied it together lying beneath her.

Then she remembered how she had fallen asleep. Hassan must have carried her to bed. Making herself think about it dispassionately, she knew it had been the best thing that could have happened. With that long yesterday pressing upon her, that strange, haunting camel ride through a vast, almost magical desert, and then... She thrust away from her what had happened in this room... on this bed.

The room now, the space about her was empty. Neither Hassan nor Mustapha were in evidence. She went to rise and slip from the bed, and then there was a noise. Soraya must have been sitting just beyond the hooked-back flap, for she came inside on hearing the small movement.

With the memories of last night colouring the entire place, Alicia looked sharply at the face smiling at her. But all she could discern was a friendly countenance as Soraya said, 'Breakfast is ready when you are, lady.'

'Breakfast?' Alicia sent a glance through the opening. From all she could see of the low horizon through the further opening, the sun must have been up for some hours. She said a little breathlessly, 'What time is it?'

'Just after nine o'clock, lady. So dress and have breakfast.'

Making herself speak, Alicia asked, 'Where is the lord Hassan?'

'He is working with the water. You can go out, but must eat first, he said.'

Knowing she would get from Soraya only what she had been told to say, Alicia stood upright. She walked, if a little shakily, to the minuscule bathroom and quickly showered. She didn't want the smell of sandalwood lingering about her body. However, another pristine white towel was handed to her, so, shrugging, she thought, Oh, well, I'll be at the hotel in Luxor tonight, and their towels don't have the aroma of sandalwood.

Back in the big tented bedroom, Alicia saw with relief that her own clothes were lying folded and clean upon a chair. Climbing into them, they gave to her the feeling and security of more familiar surroundings. Moving over to the dressing-table to comb her hair into the fair, shining smoothness it normally showed, she gazed searchingly at the face reflected back at her. Did it look the same after last night's trauma? She didn't know. What had happened?

Sighing deeply, she turned and went through to the living-room tent. A place was set for her at the table and Mustapha was standing just outside speaking to someone. He came in as she entered, saying, 'Good morning, Miss Seacombe. Your breakfast is here. I hope you like your eggs medium, not hard, not soft, because I really have to tell you,' he said smiling his familiar smile at her, 'that boiling eggs is not one of the things I do best.' He stood, holding a chair for her.

As she had looked at Soraya, so she gazed at this man. And, as the woman had done, he presented only the same manner to her that he had used all along. He had removed a linen napkin off two eggs, some golden toast, and was now pouring tea for her from a small white porcelain pot.

She smiled at him, the radiant smile she so seldom used, and said, 'Thank you, Mustapha.'

However, as he was on the point of departure, she asked carefully, because he as well as Soraya would only tell her what he was told to, 'Will we be leaving for Luxor soon, Mustapha, or at some later time today?'

He halted, but she thought he would have liked to carry on. However, he half turned back, saying, 'I don't know, Miss Seacombe. The lord Hassan will tell you.' He departed.

'Yes, he probably would in his own good time,' muttered Alicia tartly, and viciously cracked off the top of an egg. She ate it all, and also the second one, finishing with the toast and marmalade. She couldn't remember when she had been so hungry, but then the long day yesterday during which she had eaten hardly anything at all gave the answer.

Rising from the table, she sauntered to the entrance, but found before she arrived there that Soraya was beside her saying, 'You can go anywhere, lady, but you must stay on paths. We have bad scorpions here. Dangerous to be bitten.'

Alicia laughed, replying, 'Well, we have bad snakes in Australia, Soraya, so I don't think I would be frightened of a little scorpion.'

Soraya shook her head. 'Bad things,' she said. 'The lord Hassan said to tell you keep on paths—although he knows you have proper shoes.'

'Does he so?' muttered Alicia. He knew too much altogether. She went outside.

Oh, of course! Ali was there, leaning against the trunk of a palm tree beyond the path meandering past Hassan's quarters. He bowed his head slightly to her, then levered himself upright. Alicia stood gazing about her, and against her will thought that it was beautiful. The big tent she had just emerged from and another large one beside it were the only dwellings at this end of the oasis. And against a sky of such deep blue that it was indigo, the clustered palm trees enclosing them sent their branches reaching to the empty heavens.

A shout echoed through to what was almost a hush where they stood, making Alicia wonder where the people that inhabited this place were. She turned on her heel and strolled along the beaten track with her guard—or whatever—twenty or so paces behind her. How stupid she thought—who would need a bodyguard here in Hassan's own back yard?

Two young boys came running, and pulled up before crossing the path on catching sight of her. She smiled at them. At least they would have no reason not to smile back at her. They didn't, grinning hugely with white teeth gleaming from the coffee-coloured faces. Not as dark as some Arabs were, thought Alicia, moving on.

Walking on past tents positioned in their own clusters of palms at the other side of the path, when abruptly she found she was among what looked like a working bee. Men, their jibbahs hiked up, were digging, concrete was being poured—and Hassan was there. He seemed almost as dirty, even though wearing khaki trousers and shirt. In the centre of all this was the reason for the existence of the oasis. An oval lake of water.

She stood watching, fascinated. Ali had moved up closer to her, but she took no notice. Were they trying to extend that lake? she wondered, on seeing the concrete wall they were building yards from it further back all around. A young man came running, yelling out, not even seeing her, and hastily Alicia stepped back. Sand was sliding, men were calling, and Ali said sharply, 'Come to stand back, lady.' She thought he would have liked to have taken her by the arm and pulled—but didn't dare. She jumped back.

Then she heard Hassan's voice speaking loudly in Arabic, and again almost immediately in English. That other young man must be English, and she thought also that nothing could have gone terribly wrong, for the men were laughing.

Then the two khaki-clad males were up beside her, and her abductor was saying, 'This is Miss Alicia Seacombe, Harry—my fiancée. She has come to see if she could manage to like staying here sometimes while I am working. Harry Jennings, Alicia.'

She couldn't even make herself close a mouth which had fallen open as she looked up at his face: classical certainly, handsome absolutely, dirty yes, but what was showing to her was only a granite hardness.

'Hi, Miss Seacombe,' a young voice was greeting her. 'It's good that we are both here to find out something. I hope you're as lucky as I am, because I'm going home with the most tremendous data. My boss will be so delighted that I hope he will bring me out with him when he comes to see Sheikh Hassan again.'

Her mouth closed now, Alicia yet knew she wouldn't dare to disagree publicly with Hassan. She did say, smiling, 'I'm sure if it is about the Sheikh Hassan's subject of water, he will be delighted to have you come back. But for now I have come to see him about another journey.' With a face and expression she tried to make as hard as the one he was showing, she told him, 'I'm sure you know the one I am speaking about.'

Carefully ignoring her words, Hassan was speaking in his turn. 'Harry's boss is Professor Davidson from Cambridge, and he has lent me Harry for only a few weeks, so you can imagine how rushed we are.'

She didn't want to talk to him about any damned engineering project. She wanted to know when she was going home. She didn't want to think, either, about other words he had used when introducing her. So she was beginning to speak carefully, when again she was interrupted.

'We have a small problem, Alicia, which will keep me here until lunchtime, so you might like to go and inspect our camel herd until then.'

Camel herd? He must be mad! She wasn't going to allow her mouth to fall open again, so she said flatly, 'I really don't think so. I know nothing about camels.'

'Oh, of course, horses are your interest, aren't they? Still, they tell me you and your camel found quite an empathy for one another on the way out here.'

Teeth clenched, she went to answer, and saw the glinting piratical gleam that sometimes came to colour those emerald eyes. She also saw all the working men standing round, and noticed too that not one of them looked at her. Well, he might laugh at her, but she wasn't in the mood to laugh back. So she did the next best thing, and, unclenching her teeth, said, 'Yes, thank you, I would love to see the camels. Which way do I go?'

Hassan laughed outright, the sound making her own eyes fly open. This was the man she had known before—not the one who had come out of the night into the tent last evening.

She turned her back on him and walked to the path even though not knowing which way to go, her mind blank with remembering the first few minutes of his coming. A voice said, 'This way, lady.'

Oh, of course, Ali understood some English. He would have heard about the camels. So she went 'this way' beside him, and felt the breeze rustling the palm fronds far above her head cool her hot cheeks.

The oasis appeared larger than she had first thought, but even so they soon came to a large roped-off area, and, arriving closer, despite herself Alicia gave a small cry.

There must have been forty or more animals there, and they looked different to camels she had seen in pictures. These were pale and looked almost elegant. Up close, one came towards the fence with a tiny baby one trotting beside it.

'No...!' Ali was exclaiming sharply as she went to pat it. 'The mother bite you...' Then, pausing as if trying to find words in English, he went on, 'Camel's bite make you sick.'

'Like those of horses, I expect,' she replied, then continued, 'There are a lot, Ali. What are they used for in all this vast emptiness?' Alicia gestured to where the dunes went on and on.

'These are racing camels, and half of them are to go to an army camel core. The others are used for patrolling.'

'Patrolling...' It seemed an unlikely idea. Ali, however, didn't elaborate, and said quickly as if changing the subject, 'There, that is the one you rode last night.'

She looked at it. As far as she could see—unlike horses—they all looked the same. Elegant, haughty beasts, with long, thin legs that seemed as if they would break with the least bump.

Walking back, for the first time since she had met him, she felt herself comfortable with Ali. Through the trees on the return journey she heard chanting, and saw a ring of children apparently being taught. They looked all boys, and she thought, Yes, that would be right.

Passing the area about the water hole—or lake, or whatever—Alicia saw that they were still working. She didn't stop. She did get a surprise, though, upon entering the large tent. Hassan was there, seated at the desk speaking into a radio. He had showered and for the first time she saw that normally smooth hair dishevelled, with a heavy wet swath lying across his forehead. His clothes were as they always were, whatever kind he was wearing: immaculate. This time he had on jeans and a white silk shirt, sleeves rolled up and the top buttons left undone.

Alicia went to speak, but he held up a detaining hand as he listened to a voice speaking quickly. So she turned sideways, leaning against the tent pole, gazing out upon the forest of green palms. Ali was there, but standing well back on the other side of the path. She waited, then, when only silence echoed in the space about them as both voices stopped, she turned back into the room.

'Sorry about that, Alicia, but I was speaking to an army colonel, and as it was a bit urgent he wouldn't have appreciated being asked to wait. Did you see the camels?'

'Yes, I did see the damned camels, but that——'

'Oh, no, they are not that sort of camels. They are rather special, the animals we the ben Amarna breed. Any Arab would probably give his soul to own one...'

'Well, I wouldn't give my soul to own one, and you are only being facetious, Hassan. Now, I have an important question—no, two questions—to ask. The first is——' she tried to speak rationally, even politely '—when are you taking me back home, back to Luxor? I expect it will have to be later this afternoon to avoid the blazing heat of the day. But what time...?'

'Yes, when we do go, we will do so to avoid the heat of midday. Probably starting just before dawn. Still, I am afraid that won't be until three days, four at the latest...'

'Three days! You must be mad. What am I going to do here for three whole days? I am not staying!'

An eyebrow went up, and his face was suddenly the countenance she had seen at the hospital in Cairo. Haughty, impatient, as if being annoyed by some irritating insect. 'I am afraid,' said a voice with the imperiousness which matched that expression, 'you will have to. If you remember...' The voice paused, and both it and the expression on that face before her changed as he resumed speaking. 'I did mention once before the time-slot of three or four days. Well, that still applies— even if they might not be used for the purpose intended then.'

'You are mad,' she reiterated, looking at him aghast. She understood what he had said, and felt her cheeks go hot when remembering exactly where those words had been spoken to her—and the tone of voice he had used.

'No, I am not in the least mad. Young Harry out there——' a hand gestured backwards to where the water was '—is a very bright young lad, and I am lucky to have him—even if only for three more days. So, as my work is to me very important, I will not have it interrupted...in any way.'

'You and your work; what about my life? You have interfered with that. I want it put right straight away. I want to go back to Luxor today!'

'Yes, well, everyone has wants which are not always available to them, and have to carry on with their lives with what is presented to them.'

'*You* might have to do that! *You* might believe in this Kismet thing. I don't! I want to leave here and go back, please, Hassan...'

'I need these three days...'

'You can have them. You can send me back with Ali, or with Mustapha...'

'I can do no such thing! I, a sheikh of the ben Amarna, allowing a...a guest of mine to be sent away as if of no account. Whether they are my own sentiments or not, of course I can't. Don't be stupid, Alicia.' The entire attitude, and certainly the tone of that voice, forbade any argument about the subject at all.

Frustrated, almost in tears at being up against the un-yielding force of a granite wall which she knew now could not be dented, wondering shakily how she was going to put in three days here, in these surroundings, in this tent, with that man, suddenly brought another matter to worry about in this whole stupid affair.

She asked as curtly as she could manage to do so, 'Why introduce me to Harry as your fiancée...?'

'What would you have had me introduce you as?' With a voice just as curt Hassan interrupted her, then continued on, but in that grating silken tone she hated, 'Would you have preferred me to say, in the modern phraseology, this is my live-in girlfriend, or alternatively this is someone I picked up and who has come out here to live with me for a few days. Which would you have preferred?'

Furious, squeezing back the tears which were trying to spill out, she said shakily, 'Oh, God, how I hate you...' and, turning, walked quickly into the bedroom.

In the dimness of it, uncaring where she was stepping, Alicia nearly went head over heels as her foot struck heavily against an obstacle in her path. She glanced down, not even thinking about where she was, her consciousness taken up with the words, the action of just a minute ago out in the other room.

Then what she was looking at did register. She gazed at not one but two of the obstructions resting upon the floor. She swung round, panicking... to confront the man out there. However, walking on silent footfalls, Hassan had followed her and was already standing in the aperture.

Tears dried, apprehension taking their place, she stammered, 'That is *all* my luggage... How did you get it? What has happened to Aunt Em? She wouldn't let you... If I am to go home, why have you had my luggage brought here?' She said again, 'What has happened to my aunt?'

'Use whatever common sense you have, Alicia. Nothing has happened to your aunt. When I decided to bring you here, I planned to put you straight on to the plane at Luxor afterwards... hence your luggage! Your aunt quite accepted that you would be eager to see the far desert. She knows my writing. She also knows I am of the ben Amarna. Why should she worry?'

'Yes indeed, why...if only she knew,' answered Alicia stung. And then said for the second time in so few minutes as she watched him laughing at her, 'God, how I hate you...'

'Very well, I accept that. But you will still have to put up with me for those days. Although...' as she wasn't looking at him she didn't see lids fall over those mag-

netic eyes, allowing only the merest gleam to show
'...although,' he was repeating, 'you can make that
probably only two days, because I could have to be away
all day tomorrow—from before dawn until nightfall.'

Bringing sharply into focus the reality of where she
actually was, those words sloughed away any anger she
knew she didn't need to have. She went still and gazed
up at him. 'You're not going away and leaving me here
by myself. You can't...anything might happen. I am
not going to stay here by myself...I am not!! Her voice
trembled, going high.

'You are being stupid again, Alicia. Of course you
wouldn't be alone. Beside Mustapha and Soraya, whom
of course I would leave with you, this oasis houses a
whole community. You would be as safe here—safer,
from what one reads in the Western papers, than you
would be at home, because after all we are the ben
Amarna.

'Look,' he began again after a short pause, 'how about
seeing things sensibly? I do need to work with Harry
while I've got him. You can go and see camels groomed
and trained—just as horses are, and maybe, just maybe,
you might get your ride into the desert. You have sold
your horse and the money is on its way to Australia.
What more can you want?

'So why don't you just allow these days to slip past,
and enjoy them. The world will intrude and press its
demands upon you soon enough. Allah, don't I know!'
He wasn't laughing at her now, and, hearing those last
words, even perceiving behind them more than a hint
of strain, Alicia gave him back look for look.

'All right. Thank you, I will try to enjoy and amuse
myself here. I do know what thanks I owe to you for
Dark Shadow and Johnny, and...I will manage here if
you have to go away.'

Both his hands went up this time, palms outwards. He said, strain showing through the even voice, 'You shame me, Alicia. Now would you like to change into something cool, and we'll have lunch. Mustapha will be more than annoyed if I keep it waiting much longer.' Now it was his turn to smile, and she received the kind it was thankfully. He turned then and moved out to the other room.

Yes, she would change, she decided. She could leave the jeans and shirt for riding in. So, unsnapping the locks of her case, she rummaged for a moment then extracted a dress created from synthetic material. She shook it out; uncreased and in a pale green, it hung straight from her shoulders to below the hips from where it went on to swirl in knife-edged pleats to her knees. She changed, then added white sandals to bare apricot legs.

Before the dressing-table she combed away the tangles the breeze had put into her hair, and outlined lips again with fuchsia. Then, with her breast rising from the deep breath she took, she passed through into the living-room.

'And very nice too,' said an easy, pleasant voice, and, hearing the words it spoke, Alicia vowed that she was finished with blushing. Mustapha was present, busy with serving the food. She ate the unfamiliar dishes he set before her.

They talked about water, with Mustapha joining in. He served something she was familiar with for dessert, and, nibbling at the sticky pastry filled with nuts and fruit, she noted that Hassan was served only cheeses and long, hard fingers of toast. Mustapha placed black coffee beside his plate, then, smiling at her, he said, 'We have no fresh cream, Miss Seacombe, so I've given you tea.' Then he disappeared.

Hassan pushed back his chair, reaching into his pocket, then, pushing the chair further, he rose and walked to the entrance. He took out and lit a cheroot, drawing the smoke down deep.

'You know,' said Alicia in a voice she tried to make as pleasant as the one he normally used, 'you tell me you are a sheikh of the ben Amarna. In that case, you should surely be able to smoke in your own quarters.'

He swung round, an eyebrow going high, then, meeting only a smiling gaze, he smiled back, directly at her. However, he just said, while returning inside, 'I am smoking too many of these things just now, which is not a habit of mine.' He sat, and brought the cup of coffee to his lips, then, returning it to its saucer, he told her, 'I have to go back to work this afternoon, Alicia. Would you like to go walking around the oasis?'

'No, I'll stay here. I have two books in my case I haven't even opened, so maybe I'll read . . . or sleep off the jet lag I still seem to have.'

Finishing his coffee, he said, 'If you will excuse me, I'll change.' He rose without waiting for her assent and went through into the bedroom. She remained at the table finishing her own tea, and watched Mustapha, who had come in, clear away.

In so few minutes, Hassan was back, passing through with merely the flip of a hand. She noted the clean, pressed khakis, and remarked a little tartly, 'I know you have a generator here. You would also need to have a washing machine by the appearance of some things.'

Mustapha laughed, saying, 'No, we haven't got one yet, but who knows about the future? Still, the work gets done.'

Yes, indeed it did, she thought, remembering how her own clothes had been washed, pressed and returned in a night. She asked, 'Would it be in order if I lay on that couch to read, Mustapha? It is a little dark inside.'

'Of course. I will widen the flaps to allow more breeze to enter,' said this kindest of men. So Alicia went to fetch her book, then to settle upon a couch, which was no doubt meant for the relaxation of the owner of all this place.

CHAPTER ELEVEN

MOVING restlessly, endeavouring to push away that irritating noise penetrating a deep slumber which had
finally overcome her last night, Alicia burrowed closer
into the pillow.

'Lady, you must rise or the lord Hassan will go without
you. You have only ten minutes, he said.' Soraya sounded
anxious.

These words did penetrate a sleep-hazed mind, and
Alicia shot up. 'I'll be ready,' she exclaimed, and, almost
running to the bathroom, she washed and brushed her
teeth. Out into the big room, scrambling into pants and
bra, jeans and long-sleeved shirt, she sat to push feet
into the ankle-length desert boots. Then, knowing she
had to take some time for it, she used a lavish hand to
slap sunscreen over face and neck, using both hands
to smooth it in. 'There,' she told herself, and, picking
up the lipstick, outlined her lips deeply. She closed it up
and shoved it into her shirt pocket.

Soraya was waiting with her hat and a long white
garment over an arm. Probably the one she had worn
when coming out here, went the thought absently
through Alicia's mind.

She had heard Hassan enter. He came now to stand
in the aperture, and, his gaze roving over her completely, he nodded and gestured to Soraya. The white
cloak was folded around her and fastened, then the hat
with its leather ties handed across. She pulled them over
her head, but left the hat lying upon her shoulders. She
smiled across at the man, all thoughts of what had gone

before vanishing, her face, her eyes vivid with happiness, with anticipation. She said, 'See, I am ready!'

'Yes,' he answered, but his eyes were hooded, and *he* wasn't smiling. Gazing at that handsome but sombre face, she stammered, 'Is something wrong...?'

He made a gesture and Soraya slipped from the room. 'No, nothing is wrong,' he told her. 'I thought I would just ask you to forget about what has happened here——' a hand flew out in a throw-away gesture to the room about them '—and look on this day as something you have been given to enjoy.'

They looked across the separating space at one another, and abruptly Alicia knew that, yes, she would take this day and enjoy it. She would also take the coming days—the ones she had fought so hard against staying here for—and remember everything about them too, because suddenly now she knew, in an emotional flash of time, that meeting Hassan and falling in love with him was a gift she had been given. She would go home, not with regret, but taking with her the knowledge of having found something precious.

'Alicia...' He said only the one word and stopped.

She raised a dismissive hand, not wanting to hear what the tone in that one word presaged. She would make a life, and in it, among all the things she would have to do, would be the memory of this man. She would only have to see a ruin, a camel, a meal-table with a waiter who was not Mustapha serving it, sand on the beaches at home which was not a desert, and oh, yes, his tall figure, handsome face smiling at her in any one of his half a dozen different smiles, would be superimposed on them all.

There would be one subject he would not be superimposed upon, however, because it would not be taking place. She could not envisage being held in other arms,

being made love to by another body, as had once been
done. In Hassan's hands was the future of that life for
her—and he had discarded it.

Stretching between them, steel-threaded but invisible,
that cord held them together... immobile; then snapped
as, without intending it, without volition, Alicia raised
a hand to him. The man threw up both his own des-
pairingly, then turned on his heel and left.

Two camels were there waiting, and on the arrival of
the sheikh, their handlers hissing at them, they went
down on their knees. Hassan moved to stand beside one
of them, and as Alicia arrived he said, 'Take this,'
handing her a small cane or whip, then added, 'Pull your
cloak tight so you can wrap it around you. It will be
cold for a while.'

She mounted, and with her leg curled tight she
straightened and, looking at him, smiled gaily, saying,
'Thank you, Hassan.' Begin now as you mean to go on,
she told herself.

Side by side, the two animals stalked disdainfully down
through the oasis. Taking her place beside her companion once they were out in the open desert, Alicia saw
how many riders there were. She hadn't tried to make
her camel move, but found suddenly that it was careering
along at a fast loping trot.

She saw dunes faintly outlined, and, her glance going
upwards, she thought the stars didn't seem as bright as
they had done on the outward journey here, but were
still blazing like diamonds flung lavishly on midnight-
blue velvet. Abruptly realising what she was thinking—
midnight blue, not black—she turned to gaze over her
shoulder.

Yes, on the horizon to the east a faint paleness was
showing. The false dawn, she decided. She had seen it
in Australia when up early working the horses. Her

glance swinging back again, she saw the riders about her silhouetted more clearly, and even as she looked they took on distinct outlines.

Three camels away, her glance came to rest upon Ali. He grinned across at her—actually grinned at her! So he was happy too. This was probably what he normally did—not guarding some woman. So gaily she threw back her head, allowing the wind of their passing to blow against her face. Well, like Ali, she was going to be happy also.

A few minutes later, an hour, an aeon, a voice said, 'Look, Alicia.'

Startled out of just being happy, of not even thinking, of allowing this day, this moment to permeate her entire system, Alicia glanced sharply sideways. Hassan was smiling at her before turning to glance over his shoulder. She did the same.

'Oh...' she couldn't help the exclamation from escaping. The sun had not yet risen, but it was sending its presence before it. Along the horizon were streaks of crimson, of scarlet, of carmine, and abruptly they weren't only streaks, they had come together in a blanket of incredibly vivid shades of colour half the world in magic. 'Oh, it is really beautiful!' she couldn't help exclaiming again.

However, even as she gazed enthralled, a sliver of solidness had penetrated through the intense blanket of a scarlet horizon; then came a further sliver, and almost at once the sun had risen. Colours disintegrated, and only a huge golden ball was there—to begin pouring down its molten heat upon them while it remained king of the heavens.

There came a shouted command, and the riders began to fan out into a wide half-circle, the end ones so far away as to be just specks in the far distance. Every rider carried a lethal-looking rifle across his back—with the exception of her companion, who had, from what she remembered from her days in the bush, something much more deadly.

'With all this hardware you are carrying, you don't look as if you are just out on a Sunday morning's ride, Hassan,' she couldn't prevent herself from saying to the man riding knee to knee beside her.

'No, we're not. There have been rumours that strangers have been seen. So this patrol is twofold—one for us, and one for the government. Actually, though, I want to inspect this well for myself, to check its contents at this particular time of the year.'

'Perish the thought that there are strangers on your territory; after all you are the ben Amarna,' replied Alicia a little astringently.

'Yes, we are, and we like others to realise that,' was all he answered in a tone that held no facetiousness whatsoever. He turned then to glance into the distance at his far-flung line of warriors. Alicia returned to gaze out at a desert she would never forget, and to listen to the soft thump of the padding hooves, as they swiftly sent the miles behind them like the wheels of a speeding car.

Then, because she couldn't help it, her look returned to Hassan beside her, and she accepted that in this environment he looked only an Arab; dressed like one, acted like one. But . . . he had another environment too, she thought a little mutinously.

She came abruptly out of her reverie as a call came echoing. Hassan just threw up an acknowledging hand. He didn't appear upset, he didn't quicken the pace, so whatever the shout had been about it hadn't disturbed him.

The time passed; the padding hooves put the miles behind them, the desert remained vast as always, and then another call echoed. Hassan smiled across at her and said, 'Journey's end, for us, Alicia.'

Then she saw in the distance the merest outline of a foreign entity breaking the monotonous landscape around them. It still took half an hour or so to reach what she saw was one lone date palm, its trunk hoary with age, raising itself high into the heavens. Her camel was kneeling and Hassan was saying, 'Come into the shade and rest for a while.'

So she walked into the shade and stood rubbing the cramp from her leg, sorry for the women through all the ages who had had to ride side-saddle. The men were laughing as they brought up water from the well in a small container. Thirst quenched, it was the the camels' turn. Then it was her turn. Hassan uncapped a stoppered flask he had taken from his saddle-bag and, filling a cup brought it to her. She accepted it, smiling at him, drank it, then held it back for more.

She received a shake of the head. 'No—allowed to, you would most likely drink it all. It wouldn't be good for you. You'll get another later on. Oh, good God...' he interrupted his words as there came an upheaval just yards from them. From out of a milling crowd of both men and animals, a youth raced free. *He* wasn't happy, but the men were doubled up laughing at him.

'What was it?' she asked Hassan, still standing beside her holding the flask. He was laughing also. 'Did the camel try to bite him?'

'Let's say he has learned to be more careful about them, anyway,' he told her, and held out her further ration of water. He moved away then, and was immediately surrounded by older, bearded men whose laughter had ended. They conferred, one squatting down to draw a map in the sand. Then, with a flurry of movement, they were remounting, and in a few short minutes only the thudding of their departing hooves disturbed the airwaves about them.

It seemed they were to remount also, she and Hassan and the four remaining men. They set off homewards, with two bodyguards on either side. Ali was not one of them.

The journey back appeared faster then the outward one had been. There came a smudge upon the horizon and the camels quickened their pace even further, and one minute they were in searing heat, the next under the sparse shade of the outer palms. Then the oasis proper was sending its shade and coolness around them, and the camels were kneeling—and her ride was over.

'Shower and change, Alicia, then Mustapha will give you lunch. I am going straight back to work,' she was told by a man whose attention was elsewhere. She went to speak, but Hassan had turned, flipping a hand in farewell.

She ate lunch by herself; she also ate dinner by herself. Apparently one rider had come back early, and Hassan had stayed behind waiting for the remainder to return. So she had her meal, and waited ... Then undressed and went to bed with her book. She had heard him later, on the radio with his voice going on and on. She had switched out the light. She had fallen asleep.

There was golden sunshine when next she became aware of the world, and with gathering wakefulness she knew that this was her last day here. Tomorrow at dawn she was to be taken back to Luxor. So, doing things as the owner of this place wanted them done, she rose and had Mustapha serve her breakfast.

Lingering over it, Alicia wondered if she should return to her book and read, or go strolling around outside.

Well, of course, she wasn't going to just sit and read, so, catching up a hat, she walked outside, collected her bodyguard and began strolling.

She went towards the further end of the oasis. She wanted no part of that working area. There were young date-palms growing on the outskirts here, and she wondered if they had been planted to extend this homeland, or were just a natural phenomenon.

As she bent down to retie a loose shoelace, her arm brushed the low frond of a small palm. She felt the sting and cried out. The youth behind her ran, and she stood there pointing. His heavy sandal-clad foot came down and crushed the small scorpion, but he didn't come back to ask or console. He was off running... and shouting at the top of his voice.

The next thing she knew, Hassan had her in his arms and was running also—towards their own tent. She began to struggle and say that it was not much, but was immediately silent on hearing the viciousness of the tone replying to her.

However, someone else must have gone running. Mustapha was waiting with a white box already opened, his face showing his anxiety beneath the bronzed brown. Hassan sat her down abruptly, picked up scissors and slashed across her shirt, her bra straps, to expose her arm completely. Even while doing so, he motioned Mustapha towards the radio.

Then, bandaging her arm as tightly as he could across where the tiny sting showed, he reached for the hypodermic syringe already laid out and broke open a small glass ampoule.

Completely amazed at all these goings on, Alicia only looked at him, looked at the cruel face surfacing from out of another time, another culture, and remained silent. She turned her own face sideways when he took hold of her upper arm. She felt the needle go in. Then, as if with this occurrence, the pace around her slowed down.

'Was it a big one?' asked Hassan.

'No, I don't think so,' she was beginning to answer, her voice shaking a little. She had not been anxious at all about being stung; it was what was occurring now that made her frightened. However, she went on more positively, 'It wasn't.' And felt, rather than heard the deep breath which made his chest move sharply.

'Is it...' she began to ask.

'Yes,' he told her, but his hand had come out to clasp hers tightly. 'They are dangerous, but that thing could have been only young. Their nests are being disturbed because of our work.' He turned quickly as a shadow darkened the opening. Her young bodyguard was there, holding out his hand.

Hassan's Arabic came sharply, then more mildly as, turning to her, he said, 'Look, Alicia, it was only a baby one. Now, you have been given something to work against the poison, but you might have pain. I'll be with you all the time until we get to Cairo...'

He turned away without completing the sentence, but, seeing the expression his face held, Alicia said quickly, 'It doesn't matter, Hassan. Whatever happens, it doesn't matter...' She knew she had to change that look somehow.

'Yes, it does matter,' he was beginning, then turned away as a voice echoed sharply from the radio and he turned to answer it. His tone, curt, demanding, answered just as sharply, then seemed to be repeating some sentence. Words went back and forth for a few quick seconds, then with a swift movement Hassan flicked a switch.

He gave curt orders to an older man who had come to stand behind the youth, and who went away quickly. He said then to Alicia, 'I've got a military helicopter coming. It is big and fast.'

With her hand clasped tightly in the hard one holding it, she allowed the slow minutes to drag by. Yes, there was pain, but she could handle that. What she couldn't handle was her breathing, which took so much effort. Hassan moved a little, but only to allow Soraya to bathe her face, her forehead and neck with warm water.

The pain jumped for an unexpected moment, and her hand clenched, but it passed and she went to lean back. Hassan pulled her sharply upright. 'You are not going to sleep,' he told her in that vicious tone, 'even if you think you want to. Do you hear me? I am telling you that no little scorpion is going to get you.'

Mustapha and Soraya had gone away, Soraya into the bedroom where faintly Alicia could hear her moving about. Then Mustapha was back. He said, 'Should I give her this, Hassan?' And even far back in a mind that wasn't with-it she still noticed that he had said only Hassan, not Lord Hassan.

However, all she actually heard properly was Hassan saying, 'I don't know!'

'I don't expect it will do any harm. It is sweet and hot. It might help her metabolism,' replied Mustapha.

She knew she was trying to smile at both of them, but didn't know if she wās succeeding. Then Mustapha's arm was around her shoulders, and she was trying to drink hot, sweet tea.

But abruptly the room was receding and Hassan's voice seemed to be coming from a long way away. Her face being slapped jerked her upright and brought the room back into focus. 'You are to stay awake and talk, do you hear me?' Hassan was telling her once again in that frighteningly unfamiliar voice.

She tried to smile back, but she didn't try to talk. She found her breath too hard to come by. Then her mind was registering a sound she had heard once before. That enormous noise which had once preceded a furious Hassan coming to her from out of the night.

Soraya was folding the white cloak about her slashed clothes. Then, swung up into strong arms, she was carried through the searing heat of midday into the coolness of the great helicopter.

Even afterwards, Alicia couldn't remember very much of the succeeding events. She did remember hospital corridors which seemed to go on forever, while she was trying to get air into a body that felt strange. She also remembered a voice saying as she felt a needle being injected, 'There, that should help.'

She had nodded happily, and in a thankful whisper said, 'Yes, it does.'

Submitting to different needles, then another injection, and more aware now, Alicia glanced around for the presence she wanted to see. Hassan *was* there, but standing further back. She smiled at him carefully. She had never seen him other than immaculate. Standing there, he was filthy. He must have been wading in that lake of water back at the oasis. She smiled again.

As if the doctor had just noticed that glance, and the man to whom it had been directed, he said, 'You really shouldn't be in here, you know. You look as if you would be carrying all the germs of Cairo upon you.' The voice suggested that the man leave, and at once.

'Any germs I might be carrying, Miss Seacombe would have caught already,' replied Hassan in a tone just as curt. 'Now, if you please, could you tell me if we have

got to you in time. If Miss Seacombe will be...will be...'
The voice, curt no longer, stopped.

They gazed at one another across the bed, both auth-
oritative in their own sphere. Then the doctor said, in
the way doctors had a way of doing, 'I can't give you a
complete answer until I have the tests back, but I think
yes...'

'Yes...?' The one word came across as carefully as
Alicia had managed to smile.

'Oh, yes, I would imagine so,' murmured the doctor,
his hand upon her wrist. 'However, I do really think you
should go. There are things we need to do.' He gestured
to the sister standing by the foot of the bed.

Yes, there were things that had to be done, Alicia
found out later when, after a last look at her, Hassan
left. She knew she was much better than she had been,
but she still felt strange. Washed, she found a nightdress
being slipped over her head and, a little astonished, saw
that it was her own.

White-coated men came in and out, and there were
low-voiced consultations. The doctor was there, fingers
on her pulse every few minutes. Then, all of a sudden,
the room around her was blessedly quiet. She had been
banked high with pillows, and said drowsily, 'I feel tired,
but Hassan told me I must not go to sleep.'

'We have got you banked up and filled with antivenom
now, so just do what comes naturally, Miss Seacombe.
I'll be here all the time, checking,' said the middle-aged,
competent-looking sister.

So, upon her pillows, Alicia dozed on and off, with
the doctor as well as the sister coming in every few
minutes to check. Then it wasn't a white-coated figure
who entered next time. The first she knew of it, however,
was when the sister said, 'You can't bring those in here,

Sheikh Hassan. We are trying to regularise this girl's breathing.'

Alicia opened her eyes to flowers... Armfuls of them. She laughed, and, if it was not her normal laugh, it was a sort of a one. She said, 'Oh, back to normal, I see.'

'You will have to take them out, now that our patient has seen them,' said a voice which even Hassan could not gainsay. The flowers disappeared. Hassan didn't. He came and sat on the bedside chair, with the sister going to sit by the window. He said, almost grinning at her, 'You are looking almost yourself again.'

'Of course I am. Who cares about a little old scorpion's bite,' she began but found she couldn't speak as much as she would have liked to do. However, she could think. And she thought that they *were* back to normal as she looked at the tall, immaculate figure, the outstandingly handsome face.

However, Hassan wasn't taking in that gaze. He was looking at her, all over her, and was asking softly, 'You are feeling better, aren't you?'

'I'd better be, with needles, and blood-tests, and doctors arriving in here every few minutes! Of course I am. Can I also say that you look different now from my last view of you—dress-wise, I mean?' It was Alicia almost grinning this time.

'We have a house here. I live there when I am in Cairo.'

'I suppose you have a house everywhere,' he was answered a little tartly.

'Well, practically everywhere,' replied a silken voice. An eyebrow went up and emerald eyes glinted amusement at her. 'I see *you* are getting back to normal also,' he told her.

'Still, I am going to have dinner here in bed, while I expect you are going out dining among all your Cairo

friends. Your clothes certainly give that appearance.' She
hadn't meant to say it. Why did she behave like this?

'Of course I am going dining, to the best restaurant
in Cairo. I have a book with telephone numbers—isn't
it called a little black book?' He looked at her lying there
and added, 'Don't be stupid, Alicia. Of course I am not
going out dining. I have a mountain of work to get
through—my own, as well as a session with the army
which I could well do without—especially tonight.

'And even if I hadn't all those things to do, I wouldn't
feel like going out dining anyway.' His hand reached out
to touch hers lying against the white quilt, but it drew
back sharply. He said, 'I have just had a talk with the
doctor, and you may be allowed home after the specialist
has been—if you promise to do exactly...'

'I will!'

'You don't know what I am going to say.'

'Yes, I do. And I will!'

'You should be careful of giving wild promises, you
know.'

'It was not a wild promise, Hassan.'

'OK, then. I also have a promise for you. I will have
your aunt here by tomorrow afternoon. For Allah's sake,
calm down...' Hassan glanced swiftly across his shoulder
at the sister. 'You will have me thrown out if you show
the least breathing increase, or your blood-pressure goes
up.'

'Oh, phooey. However, you did mention the word
"stupid" before, and that I really am not. I want to get
out of here, so I will be careful to do everything as I
should. Where will I go? Back to the Cairo Hilton, I
expect?'

Hassan waved away her question, only saying, 'All
right, you be careful, then, and don't let either of those
things get out of control when Johnny comes to see you

tomorrow morning. He had to be forcibly prevented from coming today.'

'Oh, is his leg out of plaster? Did you see him? Is he OK?'

Hassan threw up both hands. 'I had to give my solemn word I wouldn't get you the least bit upset, or I wouldn't have been allowed in here. Now just look at you. I'm going before they throw me out. Goodbye Alicia.' He went, just like that. Alicia couldn't believe it.

Couldn't believe, either, the sister's scowl when she came back to the bed and took up a wrist. She told her patient after a few short seconds, 'Now you settle down, Miss Seacombe, or we'll get the doctor in to give you a needle.'

CHAPTER TWELVE

'REALLY, Hassan, this is too much!'

Up went an eyebrow, a haughty expression coming to mar the classical profile presented to her. 'Explain please?' said her companion.

'You said you had a house in Cairo. You didn't say a palace.'

'It was a palace once, but my great grandfather allowed it to go to rack and ruin. Now there, my dear Alicia, was a man you wouldn't want to know about.'

'Wouldn't I?'

'No, you would not, and you are not going to be told. So don't look at me with that so enquiring, innocent gaze. My stepmother refurbished it when she married my father. They have that side.' Hassan pointed across the forecourt. 'Yusef and I have apartments in the middle, and my uncle...' The voice paused for a moment then continued, 'has the ones you are going to occupy. Come along.'

Alicia held back, gazing at him, 'You have that funny look in your eyes. Is there something wrong about those rooms? Or... are you just planning something?' she wanted to know.

Hassan caught hold of her hand, but only used measured steps towards the stairs going up to the second storey. The big heavy door barring their passage gave way to merely light fingertips, as again so did the opening in intricate iron railings that ran from floor to ceiling. Inside them, she halted abruptly, saying only, 'Oh...'

One side of the huge open room had three thin slits of pointed windows with two paintings of this country hanging between them. Not of the Pyramids; not even of the Nile—but of the desert. One of the morning awakening; the other, as she had seen it herself, of its inclines and hollows lending itself to the illumination of only starshine. 'Oh,' she exclaimed again, and turned to meet a lop-sided smile on the face opposite.

'I didn't expect you to notice them first, but I knew you would like them when you did. They are by a famous artist,' said Hassan.

'You wouldn't need to tell me that,' was all Alicia answered, still standing there gazing.

'Now, how about the rest of the place,' began her companion, so she turned obediently to look at it. She almost said 'oh' again, but didn't. She could, however, have been stepping into an *Arabian Nights* environment—without the rugs. There were no carpets. There were tiles, though, gleaming and beautiful, which spanned the entire floor. There was heavy carved furniture, and low couches, giving a brilliance to the room with their vividly coloured cushions scattered every which way.

Above her, there were shining brass lamps, hanging from equally gleaming chains. There was a view through wide arched windows across a terrace and beyond—the river.

She said, still gazing about her, 'Was the word "palace" used a short time ago?'

'I don't know if the word palace was used before, but I have something to say to you now. What would you think of being married to me?'

Alicia heard the words, heard the unlikely composition of them. He hadn't said, 'I love you, Alicia. Will you marry me?' He had used words which might have been construed as entering into some business contract.

She said, 'It depends!'

'Tell me upon what it depends.' The handsome face opposite her had closed up, lids falling half shut.

'Oh, Hassan, look, this is silly. You say those words to me out of the blue. You also once told me you were not going to be involved in a situation such as this. You don't even sound as if you want me.'

'Oh, I want you all right, but...'

'Yes, I acknowledge that,' Alicia's interruption paused for a moment then continued, 'Some of our love scenes showed even me that. But is that sort of wanting enough to enter into marriage?' Was she being stupid? she wondered. It didn't matter why he was asking her; she should just say, Yes, thank you, I think I would be happy about being married to you. But she knew she couldn't.

She told him, 'You must know how I feel about you. You must know that more than anything I want to be with you. Being made love to by you...but I would always wonder if you had only asked me out of guilt because one of your horrible scorpions bit me.'

'Oh, yes, now we come to the word "guilt". I shouldn't have had you brought out to the Far Oasis in the first place. And, having you there, I shouldn't have behaved as I did. However, that scene in my bedroom brought one thing into clear perspective. It showed me that the ben Amarna, the different cultures, had no substance for me any more; that without you my life would be dust and ashes. But you wouldn't even look at me, didn't even want to speak to me. I knew you were quite genuine when you said all you wanted to do was go back home...

'So that is why I had you come on the patrol. I wanted to bring back ordinary, mundane things.'

Pushing aside for the moment other words he had spoken, she said, 'If you think that that camel ride out into the desert was ordinary, mundane, you really don't know me, Hassan.'

The man opposite raised a dismissing hand at her interruption. 'I didn't mean ordinary in that sense,' he told her, 'I meant the other things which happen in the world. What I did was completely out of character too. Can you imagine what my men thought of my taking a female on a patrol—especially on one which this time we had reason to believe might not be just routine?'

It was Alicia who raised a dismissing hand this time while she said, 'Oh, but your men would never think about anything you did, would they? They just only obey your orders.'

Hassan's hand went up, acknowledging the hit, but he was smiling across at her more naturally now.

'Still, never mind that,' went on Alicia, not as sure of her ground now. 'You did say something about dust and ashes...'

'Would you believe I meant them?' replied Hassan.

'I can't see how I could, after... after...' She was stammering now, thinking of what those words meant.

'Look, Alicia, I don't know how to behave this morning. I have been told that you must have absolute rest and quiet for two weeks—to allow your metabolism to get back to normal...'

'Do you mean to tell me that you presented that cold-blooded proposal because you were frightened I might collapse with shock if it had been couched differently? I might well have done, but the cause would not have been because of any old scorpion's venom still in my system. It might have been... It would have been...'

She moved across the few paces separating them; she did something she would never have thought herself capable of—had never in her wildest dreams imagined herself doing. Oh, yes, she *had* dreamed of a love scene, but of one with Hassan making love to her. Never of herself doing what she was going to do.

On tiptoe, she reached hands to his shoulders and set her lips to move across the sculptured ones almost level now with her own. There came no reaction; the man's body against which she was leaning remained rigid, not responding at all. Frightened now of what she had done, her resolution disappearing, she couldn't prevent her body from collapsing.

An arm went round to hold her, an arm more rigid than his lips had been. Another arm went to join it, and she was being held loosely between them. Then, as if finding some kind of answer in her expression, in her whole attitude, the loosely held arms around her tightened, one to spreadeagle low upon her back, bringing her body into his, length against length, with hollows and curves fusing one into the other.

She found herself being kissed, not with the butterfly touch she had used on him just a short moment ago, but with demand, with intent, with slow, heartbreaking caresses which were dragging her very soul into another dimension. Then the lips had shifted, hesitating for a brief moment at the corner of her mouth before beginning to travel downwards. Her head, hair a golden cascade falling across the sleeve-clad arm, was arched backwards, leaving the silken smoothness of throat and breast open to his every wish.

Deep inside somewhere she felt the shudder that engulfed her. It only made her press even closer to the hardness of muscles and contours that was his big tense body. Then, as if that small reflex had broken through to the man, she was abruptly put away.

She heard the exclamation, but not its meaning; it echoed across to her in harsh Arabic. She shook her head, uncaring about it, only wanting to be where she had just been. But her body was a betraying entity. It went lax, sliding down against the one still enfolding it.

She was swung up and carried to the terrace, and lowered onto a long chair. Then Hassan disappeared. He was back in seconds carrying a glass of bright yellow liquid. 'Drink this,' he was telling her—and not in the pleasant voice of a host offering refreshment. He said again as she made no effort to accept it, 'I was told to see you had liquid, so drink the lot.'

Aware of his anger, aware of an almost frightening violence, her hand went out as ordered. But it was slack, and a hard one closed over it, taking it upwards to her mouth. She drank—what else could she do, with that hard hand holding the glass against her mouth. It was the same drink given to her by Mustapha on the felucca.

'All of it,' said a voice in the same tone as before. She drank the lot, and the hard hand took back the glass from her. Hassan moved away and went to stand by the railings, to gaze out over the river.

'I only wanted——' he said, then repeated, 'I only wanted to get a date set for when the two weeks the doctor mentioned were up. I never meant it to get out of hand.'

'Hassan, please,' Alicia threw out a hand to him. 'How was I to take that proposal? Knowing your views, I even thought that those last three days at the Far Oasis were your way of making them pass until I could be taken back to Luxor. Then of course there was that wretched scorpion affair.'

Hassan left the rail and came to lean against a table beside her; he said, 'I thought you were going to die, Alicia. And you told me once, when you were so ill, that it didn't matter.' He swore, and the harsh Arabic echoed back to her violently.

'Well...' Trying to get some semblance of rationality into this traumatic conversation, Alicia said lightly, gaily, 'I didn't think I was going to die, because we don't think that much of scorpions in Australia. We have so many worse things.' She pushed away from her memory how strange her body had felt at one time.

'This is not Australia, however. This is Egypt...Africa, and scorpions are very dangerous here.' Hassan went silent for a short moment, then, when he spoke again, it was also in Arabic, but in a different tone from the harsh one of before.

Alicia reached out a hand almost imploringly, only to have her companion lean further back against the table, and say sharply, 'No!'

'It's not fair. You say things I can't understand. It is rude and you shouldn't do it.'

'Should I not?' Thankfully she saw now that those magnetic eyes were smiling at her. He said, the smile now in his voice, 'I also intend to continue using that medium. I have no intention, light of my life, of uncovering all my desires and thoughts to you. Just think of the emotional blackmail I could let myself in for.'

'Light of my life,' repeated Alicia, the words coming slowly as if being savoured. She gazed across at him and said softly, 'You did say it, didn't you?'

'Did I? You know, sometimes I forget what I do say when I speak in English.' His eyes weren't just smiling now; they were glittering with that piratical gleam which sometimes issued from them when he was amused or happy. 'Still, now to serious business. Do you want to marry me?'

'Yes please!'

Hassan laughed outright. 'There—I must say that when you do do a thing you do it handsomely. So do you think you could give me an idea of what time, or which day, would suit you best?'

It was with a touch of hesitation that she asked, 'Could I think about it? I would like to talk with Aunt Em.'

'Of course... It's only that it is such short notice and there are a great many things to do. Also...' It was Hassan's turn to hesitate now. 'Would you object very much if my stepmother helped with some of the arrangements?'

'Arrangements...' Suddenly butterflies were tumbling every which way beneath her midriff. She had never thought about the actual fact of marrying Hassan. Of course she hadn't. She hadn't dreamed she would ever be doing so.

'I thought,' she said now slowly, 'I thought we would just get married. I didn't think about any arrangements.' Of course there would have to be some, considering who he was, and probably what he was. She said again more slowly, 'Where will we be married.'

He came to sit beside her on the long chair, and picking up her hand, started to gently rub at it with a thumb. He said, 'I deliberately didn't discuss my religion, because I intended to have only those few days with you, and then I would be gone. However...we will be married in the Anglican Church here in Cairo. I was christened in it.'

Hassan raised a hand to silence her interruption, then continued. 'Still, I lived out here; I was brought up out here as a Moslem, which however will not affect you. You must admit also that our meetings, our times together were not in the nature of any ordinary courtship.'

It was Alicia's turn to raise a dismissing hand this time, first trying to free the one Hassan had, but it was held tight, so she said anyway, 'What about your people, Hassan—will they... ?'

'It will make no difference. My uncle might perhaps prefer me to marry an Egyptian, but,' Hassan laughed, 'he is going to have all his time taken up with getting Yusef married. And times are changing, Alicia. I have two young sisters who are being educated in England. And my stepmother is not English. She comes from Saudi Arabia, so...'

'What?' the exclamation was forced from her. 'I didn't know you even had two sisters.'

'There are quite a few things you don't know, and that, my beloved, is something I hope to keep that way for the time being. Now, I don't expect this to be a small wedding, Alicia. For in my job, I move around in the European Community; and even more frequently among the English contingent. Still, when all this is over, we will go downriver to the ben Amarnas' main oasis. You won't mind that, will you?'

'Of course I won't. What I will mind is wondering what I have let myself in for.'

'Oh, I shouldn't imagine you need worry about that. After all, that is what I am here for.' Hassan was laughing again at her as he stroked a long finger down a cheek that was showing more than a tinge of carnation.

He went to move into the large, beautiful room, saying over a shoulder, 'Mustapha will be up directly to serve your lunch. Then, as the doctor ordered, you are to go to bed and rest.'

'I am not going to bed to rest. Don't be silly, Hassan.'

'You are going to bed. Soraya will be here to see that you do. Look Alicia, I really can't take any more worry about you. You have those blood-tests at the hospital tomorrow, and if the news is good, well, then, we'll see.'

Once again he went to walk away, then stopped to speak, but not over his shoulder. He looked directly at her, and suddenly she wished she could stand up to meet whatever was coming. He was looking like a pirate again. 'Oh, I thought you might like to know,' he was telling her, 'that this apartment was once the harem—and by all accounts was certainly kept fully occupied.'

'In that case, why waste such a beautiful setting when you could use it for yourself?' Alicia's tone carried none of the amusement showing so openly in the man's demeanour. It carried astringency. Then, gesturing about her with an outflung arm, she added, 'Having it all here at your disposal, surely you need not go to the hassle of getting married?'

'Oh, yes, I do. It was always necessary to have a senior wife. What came after was only the icing on the cake.' He was laughing openly at her now as he said, 'You really shouldn't try to cross swords with me, Alicia. I'm way beyond your league.'

Lying there on her long chair, she watched the tall, assured figure cross the gleaming tiles, open the small doorway in the scrolled railings, and disappear. She thought, lying back carefully, that it was just as well he *was* going, for she didn't feel all that well. Oh, it wasn't as bad as she had felt after that sting—but she did feel as if she had no energy at all.

She turned slightly to gaze out over the river, this famous Nile which had been the life-blood of Egypt for so many thousands of years. She smiled happily at it, but she also thought too of all the needles she had had to suffer this morning. How, after they were all finished, the door had opened and a wheelchair had been propelled in.

'You don't look very well,' Johnny had said without any other greeting. He was gazing anxiously at her.

She had grinned at the familiar face, known for always. She'd said, 'Never mind me—all your freckles are showing.' He hated his freckles, but, as he had grown older, suntan had come to cover them.

'They might be, but they'll go as soon as I get out of this damned place. Still, I never thought you would end up in here. A little scorpion . . . really, Alicia! We are a pair, aren't we?'

'Yes, but Johnny, the horses are sold, and Grandfather won't have to worry now. And neither do you, Johnny. Dark Shadow sold well so you will have your own money now—quite a lot. It will be a start for you to do what you want.'

'I know. That Sheikh Hassan came and told me last night. Not the one I first met and didn't like at all—the one who was there when you came to the hospital. So maybe we can start something together: train horses, or . . .'

'No, I don't think so, Johnny. I don't know what I'll be doing. Maybe some sort of a job, until I find what I would like.' She had been telling the truth. She really hadn't known what she would be doing, but there had been a germ of an idea far back in her mind.

She had asked, 'Now tell me about your leg. Is it getting better?'

'That specialist who was brought in says so. He's going to take off the plaster in a week. He said maybe I might be able to do without the top plaster, but not the lower one. He would know after the X-rays. You know what doctors are like, Alicia.'

No, she didn't know what doctors were like. She hadn't had much to do with them. So she had told him about the auction—suitably censored—and the way Dark

Shadow had behaved before the whole crowd. They had laughed together at other things the beautiful horse had done and she had told Johnny that Charles would love him. Then the sister had come over to the bed, to show Johnny firmly out...

She glanced up now as a shadow came to fall across her. 'Will you have lunch on a tray out here, Miss Seacombe,' asked Mustapha, 'or inside at the table?'

She looked at the man she had come to like so much, thinking that she didn't really want to get up. That she didn't really want any lunch, either. She said, 'Inside at the table, please, Mustapha.'

So she sat at a table and made herself eat some of the food placed before her. She drank two large cups of tea. Then she rose obediently and went with Soraya into a large bedroom, quite as lovely as that lounge outside. She took off her dress, and donned the short cotton housecoat Soraya handed to her. She lay down on the bed, burying her face in the pillow.

She was determined to ignore that scene with Hassan which she knew she herself had initiated—and also what they had discussed afterwards. She would not even think of what she was going to tell Aunt Em. She went to sleep.

CHAPTER THIRTEEN

'LADY, you must wake up. It is getting late.'

The words, spoken for a second time, brought Alicia upright on an elbow. Then, more fully awake, she realised what day it was. This was her wedding-day! She grinned on seeing what Soraya held. 'Are you spoiling me just for today?' she asked the girl standing beside the bed. Nevertheless, she reached for the cup of hot steaming liquid.

Alicia glanced again at the girl, named, she knew now, after another Soraya—Hassan's stepmother. She said, 'Just give me five minutes alone while I drink my tea, please.'

Soraya smiled, handing over the cup, and departed. Alicia pulled her knees up and, leaning back against the pillow, thought of the time she had first slept—no, napped—in this bed three weeks ago—and her awakening.

She had felt the bump on the foot of the bed and, startled, had raised herself up in alarm, to see the elderly lady seated there, the hat she always wore for best set aside upon the large handbag. She had flown up, throwing arms around the thin wrinkled neck.

Clasped firmly in still strong arms, she was hugged tight and then set back. 'You're crying,' said Aunt Em. 'You don't cry. The only time I've seen you in tears was when you were thrown off that wild brumby and ran a stake through your arm. You were eleven years old then.'

'I'm not crying. I'm not!' Alicia rubbed both wrists against her eyes, but the tears continued to fall. 'I'm not crying,' she said again, 'I'm just a little tired from being ill.'

She took the handkerchief held out to her, and wiped her eyes. 'See,' she said. 'I'm fine now.'

'That being so,' said the dry, caustic old voice, 'You can tell me now what everything is all about. I've met this Sheikh Hassan, both down at Luxor when calling for you, and again out at the airport just now when he came to meet me. I realise he is the handsomest man I have ever met. However, handsome is as handsome does, I've always found.'

Alicia choked. Hassan! Fancy anyone speaking about him like that.

However, her aunt was continuing, 'This has all happened so suddenly, Alicia. I want to know if you're happy about it. Because, if not, we finish it right away— powerful as the ben Amarna may well be...'

She raised a hand to stop the interruption she saw hovering on Alicia's lips, and went on, 'I remember you once saying that this man could have almost any woman he wanted. Well, experiencing his manners, his charm at the airport, just looking at him, I accept that. Still, loving you as I do, I realise you are not one of the beautiful or glamorous women who grace this world. So why...?'

'I expect it might be because he loves me,' replied her great-niece in a small voice.

'Does he?'

'He says so. Even though everything you have just said is true.'

'Do you love him?'

'Oh, yes. I think it happened outside the Cairo airport the day we arrived. Hassan, however, had no intention of repeating his father's mistake.' Here Alicia saw her aunt nod, so thought she must already know something of the story. 'He said so *and* he meant it. I thought, Aunt Em, that it was unfortunate that I had ever come to Egypt—even though the reason for my doing so was a success. One doesn't often get a girl of twenty wondering what she's going to do with a life—without love, and marriage, and family, because even that far back I knew I wouldn't want any other man holding me in his arms, making love to me. There, does that answer your question?'

Aunt Em went to rise from the bed, saying, 'Yes, I expect it does.'

A telephone rang. Both women glanced round for it. Then Alicia saw what she wouldn't have thought was a phone on the bedside table. She sat hunched up, just looking at it.

'Don't you think you had better answer it?' asked Aunt Em.

So, as if giving a far jump into the unknown, Alicia picked up the oblong top of what must be the phone. She said, 'Hello?'

'You sound strange. Are you all right?' asked a voice without any other greeting.

'Of course I am.'

'You have had your sleep. I know that...'

'How did you know? I suppose you assumed that because you ordered it.'

'I came up to check before going to the airport. Is your aunt with you now?'

Glancing across at the older woman sitting on her bed, Alicia said, 'Yes.'

'Alicia, I'm sorry to have to tell you this, but I am up to my ears in work. So would you mind having a quiet dinner with your aunt? Why don't you go out to the hospital and see that foreman of yours? I'm sure your aunt would like that. I'll have the car waiting downstairs for you in half an hour.'

She wouldn't see him tonight was the first thought that came, then she said without volition, 'What kind of work?'

A laugh echoed over the line to her. 'Actually,' said Hassan. 'It is company work, conferring with our manager here, then phone calls to all over the world. I could well do without it for the present. Tomorrow...oh, now tomorrow I will be doing work I want to do. Putting in train all those arrangements that I find are necessary for our wedding.'

She didn't answer, but the other voice continued, 'Oh, by the way, have I ever told you before that I love you?' Alicia didn't answer again. So he only laughed softly and said, 'See you soon, Alicia!' She was left sitting there with a silent phone receiver in her hand.

She glanced at the astringency in the face looking at her, but she only said, 'Hassan is snowed under with work. He suggests we go to the hospital to see Johnny, and then you and I just have a quiet dinner here. OK?'

'What are we waiting for, then? Come along and get ready.' So they had got ready and gone downstairs. The big limousine was waiting, and also waiting was a man leaning against it. Grinning, Alicia said, 'Hello, this is another Miss Seacombe—my aunt.'

Her great-aunt was given his usual small bow, then Ali ushered them into the car, as always, with silence. Alicia began to giggle, saying, 'He has been my body-guard, and I think he hated it; he would much rather have been out in the desert riding patrol.'

'I think you *must* have been sick to go on like this from one extreme to another,' said her aunt caustically.

'Yes, I actually was, but I suddenly feel fine now,' Alicia started to giggle again. Then they were pulling up before the hospital entrance, exactly beside a 'No Parking' sign. What did she care? she thought, and went up the steps. She sat happily on a chair drawn back a little from the bed, enjoying the laughter and talk of home and broken legs. The time flew, and there then came a sister saying that visiting time was over.

Downstairs and inside the car once more, they found their driver was giving them a tour of the city. Past the Pyramids, which she intended to visit one day. Past tall buildings which the sinking sun was turning into just silhouettes; then up to a dinner out here on the terrace, watching the sun paint the western bank of the Nile with crimson and scarlet.

Alicia knew that she wouldn't sleep, so she took a book and tried to read. The printed word was there, but it didn't make sense. Hassan's features were superimposed on it. She closed it up and switched out the light. Anyway, she would see him tomorrow, if only to go to that damned hospital to have tests.

And, waiting for him out on the terrace the next morning, she turned from watching the river as he came to stand just within the entrance. Her hand reached down to hold the railing for support.

'Hi, there,' he said. 'You look lovely; yellow becomes you.' Then, in a different tone altogether, he continued, 'Don't look at me like that. You're not being fair, Alicia.'

Oh, speaking of fairness, she knew who wasn't being fair! She knew she could walk along that strong invisible cord stretching between, holding them together, and then be in his arms, against his body. She walked the terrace . . . and then into the large, opulent living-room, giving the immobile man a wide berth. Picking up her small bag, she turned, saying, 'Shall we go?'

Returning no answer, he held the small gate open, then paused at the heavy wooden door, saying, 'Your aunt is not here?'

'No, she's down exploring the gardens of the harem.'

'Well, well, well…what a wasted opportunity. I could have swung you up in my arms, carried you inside and kicked shut a door, leaving nature to take its course. How about that?' Seemingly, he had dismissed the tensions of some previous emotion and was now smiling down at her, green eyes wide open.

'Oh, I don't think so, knowing you by now. There's no way you would go against a doctor's edict—if you thought he was right.' Alicia wasn't smiling; the gaze she was directing at him was ironic.

'OK. Maybe you might be just right. However, allow me to tell you, my dear Miss Seacombe, that sometimes circumstances change cases. Bear that in mind.' He opened the door, and stood back to allow her to pass.

Downstairs, she stood in the forecourt wondering why the limousine wasn't waiting there. She couldn't believe that anyone had slipped up. Hassan reached for her elbow, guiding her towards the other car standing there. She looked it over, then, gazing at the man beside her, grinned, as widely as she had ever done. 'I would never have believed it. It just isn't you!'

'But then you have never seen me—in London—in Paris—in Geneva,' replied a voice in just as ironic a tone as the one she had used only moments ago.

They drove along busy, crowded streets, through a blue and golden day, to the hospital. She had her tests; the results of which would be delivered to the Sheikh Hassan.

'Well now, would you like to meet my father and stepmother?' asked Hassan when they were back in the car.

Once again butterflies were fluttering beneath her midriff. As she remained silent, a long, tanned finger came under her chin to raise a face. 'How long have you known me, Alicia?' asked Hassan.

Alicia did reply to those words, saying, 'Just a bare week I think; seven days.'

'In those seven days, though, you would have come to know me, wouldn't you?'

'Oh, yes, I'll agree with that.'

'Then you should know that there is only one thing you need to worry about, and that is that only my wishes, my desires count! You have no need to be afraid of what my father thinks—or even what my uncle, who speaks for all the ben Amarna, thinks. Do you understand me?'

'Yes, I understand you,' she had replied a little shakily. 'But I could begin to think that it might be like jumping out of the frying-pan into the fire.'

'Oh, no, it won't be, I promise you.' A hand was lifted, the inside of a blue-veined wrist was kissed . . . slowly, then the low-slung vehicle jumped forward.

It wasn't frightening at all. She was greeted warmly by the older Sheikh Yusef who was Hassan's father. She smiled hesitantly at the lady Soraya, tall, assured, but not at all beautiful, who in so few minutes whisked here away to discuss wedding plans. Alicia only said yes or no. What else could she do about this marriage which had so many pitfalls?

So the two weeks had drifted past, for her mainly resting as she had been ordered. Escorted by the lady Soraya for the last tests—because Hassan was in England, working, he had told her over the phone, and also to bring his sisters back home—she had been informed that the doctors had given her a clean bill of health.

There had been some parties given for her—by the British and others. She had also met Sheikh Ahmed who arrived with all his entourage. She had liked the fierce old man.

Then . . . there had been the night after one such affair when Hassan had brought her home. He had said, 'I won't say goodnight yet, as I have something for you.' The large, silent room was only dimly lit by a light left burning by the entrance, and Hassan bent down to switch on a table lamp. He withdrew two leather boxes from his jacket pocket, setting one down; the other he clicked open. 'You have never mentioned an engagement ring. Did you think one was not forthcoming? Or . . . didn't you want one?' he asked.

'Of course I wanted one. I wanted to look at it on my finger and know that you gave it to me. That it meant that I belonged to you.'

'*Alicia* . . . ! And do you belong to me?

'Never mind,' he said when she didn't answer, 'we can go into that another time. For now, give me your hand.' She raised it wondering . . . wanting only something simple that she could always wear. She gazed down as she felt it slide upon her finger. It was no diamond or precious stone. It was deep blue turquoise set in heavy splayed gold.

The man said, 'I could have bought you anything, but that turquoise has been held by our people since the Pharaohs ruled Egypt. I had a jeweller copy it from one worn by a queen.'

'I'm afraid I won't be thinking of it as something once worn by a queen. I will only think that you had it made to give to me,' said Alicia a little breathlessly. 'Thank you, Hassan.' She stood on tiptoe in high-heeled sandals as she had done once before, with arms raised to slide around his neck.

She didn't finish the action. She was pulled into him, an arm going low upon her back to fit her body completely into his body. They stood fused together, while his lips claimed hers in a demand that sent nerves spiralling.

This time there was no seeking, no searching; there were just slow, heartbreaking kisses carrying her into a world holding only one want, one overwhelming need. Head lifted for a moment, he moved, to settle her back on a low couch with his body coming down to loom above her. Her loose neckline didn't impede their passage as lips found and caressed the smoothness of bare, silken skin.

Following where he led, she felt the room around her had no reality; it seemed smoke-hazed, made of gossamer. Then the man holding her so close that they were almost one entity had turned his head. 'Did I ever tell you, Alicia, that I want you? Because before heaven I do.'

'No, you never did. But you did tell me that you loved me, and as that came first, be my guest for whatever else...'

She felt the body fitting into hers like a finished jigsaw puzzle shake with that silent laughter which sometimes overcame him. Then he had sharply slid from the couch to walk out on to the terrace.

Alicia sat up...then stood. She pulled the loose blouse straight across her breasts, then tucked it back into her skirt. Running fingers through tangled, dishevelled hair, she then just waited.

It was only minutes before he returned, reaching up to switch on the light as he came. The man standing there looking at her seemed different. Of course he was, with hair more untidy than her own, falling over his forehead in damp, unruly locks. He also looked tired to death.

Unable to prevent herself, she reached out a hand. Hassan said sharply, 'No, I'm sorry. I don't even want to talk. I'm going.' And he did without even saying goodbye. She stood looking at the closed heavy door, then also left the room, leaving lights burning, and a small leather box which had been forgotten on the table.

She hadn't seen Hassan alone again. But she would see him today. Today she was marrying him. She pushed back the sheet and slipped out of bed.

Yes, indeed, she was going to marry him. She stood before the dressing-table, and thought that it was just as well the bedroom was large, with four other women beside herself in it. She said anxiously to the lady Soraya, 'I admit it is beautiful, but it doesn't feel like a wedding-dress.'

'Not one of your western sort probably, but you realise, Alicia....'

Alicia waved an accepting hand. Most of the ben Amarna wouldn't be at the church, but they would be at the reception afterwards. So she had to wear a wedding-dress that was suitable, and it *was* a lovely creation. Cut high straight across the top, the heavy white crêpe fell to her ankles in one unbroken line, its hem having a four inch band of turquoise embroidery outlining it. The sleeves also hung straight and had their own bands of embroidery using the same beautiful colour.

She wore no jewellery except...she smiled happily at her earrings. They had been in the other box left behind when Hassan had walked out on her—her wedding present. If anything was beautiful, they were! From flat oblongs of turquoise, three chains descended in alternate intricately engraved cubes of gold and turquoise, to come to rest almost upon her shoulders. Hassan must have mentioned the turquoise as it had come from their own vaults, and his stepmother had no doubt had the gown designed, for them to complement one another.

'I think it is time we went,' she said now. So the two older women went first, leaving Alicia to follow downstairs with her daughters. Someone was waiting at the entrance of the church, and Alicia placed a hand on the free arm Johnny extended to her; it didn't matter that they only walked slowly and perhaps a little clumsily down the aisle.

She had expected the church to be less than half-full. It was not! It was almost crowded. Then she wasn't looking at the church, or its occupants...she was walking to where two men stood, turned towards her, waiting. She heard the minister say, 'Dearly beloved, we are gathered here...' and thought afterwards that those words were practically the last coherent ones she could recall in an afternoon which was crowded...frenetic. She could remember hugging her aunt when it was time to go, and saying softly, 'Look after Johnny.'

She had received back her aunt's reply. 'I don't think I need to. He has more than enough looking after him now.' Turning to look, Alicia laughed. Johnny was propped against a wall and was surrounded by a bevy of young females.

Then, taking the necessary deep breath—despite Hassan's unambiguous words to her when sitting outside the hospital those few weeks ago—she walked beside him to say goodbye to Sheikh Ahmed. She gave to him the small curtsy as she had done when meeting him. He replied in very accented English, but he smiled at her, so she smiled back.

Yusef, standing a pace behind his father, spoke then—not in English, but in quick Arabic. Glancing at him, Alicia knew that, whatever it was, it had not been meant for her ears. He had the same wicked glint in those fierce hawklike eyes that came into Hassan's green ones at certain times.

Her new husband laughed out loud, and said in English, 'Wouldn't you just? Find your own bride.' Turning back to his uncle, he gave to him the Arabic greeting of deep respect, then, to Alicia's astonishment, he gave the same, if not so deep, to Yusef. They both raised a hand and replied with a short sentence in their own language.

Hassan's fingertips touched her sleeved elbow for the brief second, indicating where to go, then they were walking between men dressed in familiar colours. They stood aside, however, as someone was allowed to break through. His two sisters, flying up, didn't embrace Hassan, but put arms around Alicia and hugged her, saying, 'We are so happy to have you for our other sister.'

Alicia felt the sting of tears, but all she said was, 'Aren't I just the lucky one to have been given you two? We won't include Hassan in that, though, will we?' They giggled.

Her fingers entwined within other fingers on the familiar seat between them, Alicia asked, 'Why did you give that obeisance to Yusef? You sometimes say the most outrageous things about him.'

'Yes, I might. But that was in public. There were a dozen ben Amarna sheikhs there, and Yusef is my uncle's heir—therefore my paramount chief. Of course in public I would acknowledge it.'

'Oh . . .' was all she answered, and then saw that they were near the jetty. She almost said 'oh' again. The boat, or cruiser, or whatever, was enormous. They were met at the gangplank and she was introduced to a man in starched whites. A few paces beyond she held out a hand, saying, 'Hello, Mustapha.' He took it and smiled at her, but turned when Hassan said, 'We'll settle in, Mustapha, then have a drink out on our own deck. There is champagne ready?'

'Yes, of course.'

Hassan smiled at him, saying, 'It has been just one of those days, Mustapha, so we won't want dinner until it is cooler and we are anchored.' He turned away, telling Alicia, 'I'll go first to show you the way.' Down a few steep steps into a small corridor they went, where Hassan stopped for a moment and said, 'These are two guest-rooms, and this...is the state-room.' 'This' wasn't like a ship's cabin. It was like an opulent hotel bedroom, thought Alicia.

'There are five men aboard,' Hassan was again speaking to her, 'but you need see none of them except Mustapha. However I'm sorry I couldn't bring Soraya. You'll be able to manage without her, won't you?'

Alicia laughed, not silently, as the man before her sometimes did. She said, 'Don't be silly, Hassan. I've looked after my clothes, and washed them too, since I was old enough. Of course I can do without Soraya, except...' She stopped speaking and looked at the man who had taken off his jacket and tie, but was still standing over by the door.

'Except...?' he asked.

'I really do need the zip of my dress undone. It's not a ploy. I can get it undone for only so far. I could, of course,' she continued as he made no move towards her, 'go up and ask Mustapha.'

She saw that lopsided smile surface as he walked across to her. He turned her round and undid the tiny hook, then she heard the zip run down with a rush. 'You didn't need any instructions,' she told him a little astringently as, now opened completely, the lovely dress slithered to the floor.

'No, I expect I didn't. I have lived for thirty years, you know,' was all he answered.

Alicia stepped out of the material lying in a pool around her, then kicked off the white satin shoes. She stood there in bra and pants, not knowing whether to speak or try and find other clothes first. The man beside her remained silent and immobile.

'Did I ever tell you that I want you, Alicia?' said a voice which sounded slurred and strained.

'Yes, you did, and I remember telling you to be my guest!'

She found herself caught up and laid upon the large bed under the windows. His head came down, not to kiss her, but to caress back and forth across white mounds rising from a froth of lace. She shook her head in protest, then closed her eyes instead. There came the sound of movement, then Hassan's long body was lying beside her. He said with a voice again so slurred and shaken that she involuntarily moved closer, 'We don't need this,' and the froth of lace and nylon was discarded to the floor. 'Or this,' said that strange voice, as a scrap of silk followed it. 'Now, come with me, my beloved.'

So she did, and all the love-scenes they had had together coalesced into this moment of time. With his lips plundering their way along nerve-ends and jumping pulses, with his fingers following the trail they had broken having their own kind of magic beckoning her, she went with him.

Then her body was brought to fit more completely into the long, lean one holding her, and his kisses now were demanding...demanding... She knew she gasped once, then reality fell away and she was in a different dimension, flying...needing to grasp the magic within her reach.

And later, drifting, finding herself still clasped tightly in Hassan's arms, Alicia asked as he remained silent, 'Was the bargain to your liking, my lord Hassan?'

He raised himself up on an elbow, and said, 'Yes, the bargain was very much to the lord Hassan's liking, my beloved, and I must work very hard to see that the fact applies to you also.'

'Oh, Hassan...it does now. The only thing that worries me is...that I could do something you don't like.'

'Can I tell you that there is only one thing in this world that you can't do—and you would know what that is. Anything else...' He smiled that lopsided smile again at her. 'Be my guest!'

She knew that was all very well, but she also knew that living with Hassan would be no bed of roses. But then, what would living without him be like? She shivered! She raised a hand to stroke down a bare smooth chest, only to find it pushed sharply away. 'No,' he said.

'Sorry—I thought...' she began, and stopped as her new husband sank down beside her again, saying,

'Yes, I know what you thought, and at other times, you maybe could be right. But not today; not this evening, Alicia. Also, I expect we had better shower and make an appearance for dinner. The sun has gone. But, before Allah, I don't want to move.'

This time it was the girl who raised herself up on an elbow. She glanced at him and a frown came to rest between her eyes. She said, 'Why should you move if you don't want to? You have told me more than once that your people are only there to obey your orders. What does it matter it we don't eat till all hours—or even not at all? You look tired, Hassan.'

'Yes, I am tired. Apart from all the devious conniving I had to do to get this wedding smoothly on the road,

I haven't been sleeping. The trouble is, however, if I am here with you . . .' The words trailed off.

Alicia giggled as his two young sisters had done. 'Am I allowed to say again, "Be my guest!"?' she asked him softly.

So he came to be her guest as the slow minutes were counted away, second by second, and the deepening darkness of a coming night enfolded them. No one cared that the sumptuous meal was not wanted. Just one other person knew, as later it was all cleared away, while down in the large state-room only the slap of a passing wave against it disturbed the silence. Only a shaft of pale moonlight finding its way through the curtains saw the bronzed limbs entwined with the paleness of apricot and white.

Tomorrow was another day; this was tonight and it was theirs.

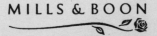

Temptation

Lost Loves

'Right Man...Wrong time'

All women are haunted by a lost love—a disastrous first romance, a brief affair, a marriage that failed.

A second chance with him...could change everything.

Lost Loves, a powerful, sizzling mini-series from Temptation starts in March 1995 with...

**The Return of Caine O'Halloran
by JoAnn Ross**

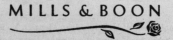

MILLS & BOON

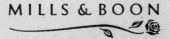

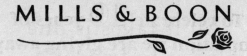

MILLS & BOON

Next Month's Romances

Each month you can choose from a wide variety of romance with Mills & Boon. Below are the new titles to look out for next month.

THE HEAT OF PASSION	Lynne Graham
SWEET SINNER	Diana Hamilton
UNWANTED WEDDING	Penny Jordan
THE BRIDE IN BLUE	Miranda Lee
FAITH, HOPE AND MARRIAGE	Emma Goldrick
PS I LOVE YOU	Valerie Parv
PARTNER FOR LOVE	Jessica Hart
VOYAGE TO ENCHANTMENT	Rosemary Hammond
HOLLOW VOWS	Alexandra Scott
DISHONOURABLE SEDUCTION	Angela Wells
TEMPTATION ON TRIAL	Jenny Cartwright
TO TAME A TEMPEST	Sue Peters
POTENT AS POISON	Sharon Kendrick
SHORES OF LOVE	Alex Ryder
DANGEROUS ATTRACTION	Melinda Cross
PASSIONATE RETRIBUTION	Kim Lawrence

To celebrate 10 years of Temptation we are giving away a host of tempting prizes...

10 prizes of FREE Temptation Books for a whole year

— **plus** —

10 runner up prizes of *Thorntons* delicious Temptations Chocolates

Enter our Temptation Wordsearch Quiz Today and Win!

10ᵗʰ All you have to do is complete the wordsearch puzzle below and send it to us by 31 May 1995.

The first 10 correct entries drawn from the bag will each win 12 month's free supply of exciting Temptation books (4 books every month with a total annual value of around £100).

The second 10 correct entries drawn will each win a 200g box of *Thorntons* Temptations chocolates.

I	F	G	N	I	T	I	C	X	E
A	O	X	O	C	A	I	N	S	S
N	O	I	T	A	T	P	M	E	T
N	B	V	E	N	R	Y	N	X	E
I	R	O	A	M	A	S	N	Y	R
V	C	M	T	I	U	N	N	F	U
E	O	H	U	O	T	M	V	E	T
R	N	X	U	R	E	Y	S	I	N
S	L	S	M	A	N	F	L	Y	E
A	T	O	N	U	T	R	X	L	V
R	U	O	M	U	H	I	A	A	D
Y	W	D	Y	O	F	I	M	K	A

TEMPTATION	ROMANTIC
SEXY	SENSUOUS
FUN	ADVENTURE
EXCITING	HUMOUR
TENTH	ANNIVERSARY

PLEASE TURN OVER FOR ENTRY DETAILS

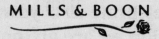

MILLS & BOON

HOW TO ENTER

10⁴ All the words listed overleaf below the wordsearch puzzle, are hidden in the grid. You can find them by reading the letters forward, backwards, up and down, or diagonally. When you find a word, circle it or put a line through it.

Don't forget to fill in your name and address in the space below then put this page in an envelope and post it today (you don't need a stamp). Closing date 31st May 1995.

Temptation Wordsearch,
FREEPOST,
P.O. Box 344,
Croydon,
Surrey
CR9 9EL

COMP395

Are you a Reader Service Subscriber?   Yes ☐ No ☐

Ms/Mrs/Miss/Mr _____

Address _____

_____

_____ Postcode _____